"I saved you. Now I need your help."

Chelsea couldn't figure out which was worse: that he was asking her to betray her coworkers, or that she was actually considering doing it. What was wrong with her?

"I can do that."

"Good." He moved, but instead of moving away from her, as she might have expected once he'd gotten his way, he moved in, closing the gap between them.

Then he leaned in and kissed her, and although she'd seen it coming, knew what he'd intended, she didn't move away, didn't stop him cold. Instead, she flattened her palms on his chest, not to push him away, but to draw him close.

And even though she knew better, damn it…she kissed him back.

JESSICA ANDERSEN

MANHUNT
in the
WILD WEST

HARLEQUIN®

TORONTO • NEW YORK • LONDON
AMSTERDAM • PARIS • SYDNEY • HAMBURG
STOCKHOLM • ATHENS • TOKYO • MILAN • MADRID
PRAGUE • WARSAW • BUDAPEST • AUCKLAND

ISBN-13: 978-0-373-88867-2
ISBN-10:   0-373-88867-8

MANHUNT IN THE WILD WEST

www.eHarlequin.com

Printed in U.S.A.

ABOUT THE AUTHOR

Though she's tried out professions ranging from cleaning sea lion cages to cloning glaucoma genes, from patent law to training horses, Jessica is happiest when she's combining all these interests with her first love: writing romances. These days she's delighted to be writing full-time on a farm in rural Connecticut that she shares with a small menagerie and a hero named Brian. She hopes you'll visit her at www.JessicaAndersen.com for info on upcoming books, contests and to say "hi!"

Books by Jessica Andersen

CAST OF CHARACTERS

Chelsea Swan—Kidnapped during a prison break, the lovely medical examiner is rescued by one of the escapees and finds herself in the middle of an undercover antiterrorist operation…but she can't help wondering if she's being played.

Jonah (Fax) Fairfax—The undercover operative has been burned badly by women in the past. Chelsea makes him want to be a better man…but he can't be that man if he wants to keep her alive during the manhunt for the escaped prisoners.

Jane Doe—Fax's contact, handler and former lover keeps him on a need-to-know basis.

Sara Whitney—Chelsea's boss and close friend, the head medical examiner will do anything to avoid scrutiny from Internal Affairs.

Al-Jihad—The terrorist leader has a far-reaching network.

Percy Proudfoot—Bear Claw Creek's acting mayor has it out for the medical examiners' office.

Seth Varitek—The FBI agent is one of Chelsea's friends, but the evidence suggests he could be involved in the terrorists' plot. Does she dare trust him?

Muhammad Feyd—Al-Jihad's second-in-command will do whatever his leader orders.

Lee Mawadi—The escapee has a serious grudge against Fax.

Chapter One

WWJBD? Chelsea Swan asked herself as she headed out to the loading dock of the medical examiner's office of Bear Claw, Colorado. The e-speak stood for *What Would James Bond Do?* and served as her mantra, though some days she replaced 007's name with some of her other favorite fictional spies: Jason Bourne, Ethan Hunt, Jack Bauer and the like.

Regardless of who she was trying to channel on a given day, the mantra meant one thing: don't be a wuss. On the scale of fight or flight, Chelsea fell squarely in the "flight" category, which wouldn't be such a big deal if another part of her didn't long for adventure, for the sort of danger she read about and watched on TV, and experienced secondhand through her bevy of cop friends.

She'd gone into pathology because she'd wanted to be near police work without actually carrying a gun, and because she liked medicine, but didn't want to be responsible for another human being's life. She was good at fitting together the clues she found during an autopsy, and turning them into a cause of death. She liked the puzzles, and the knowledge that her work sometimes helped the families understand why and how their loved one had died. Occasionally she'd even even assisted the Bear Claw Creek Police Department in finding a killer, and the success had given her a serious buzz.

Most days the job was rewarding without being actively frightening. Then there were days like today, when even James Bond might've hesitated. Chelsea figured she was entitled to some nerves, though, because while she was certainly no stranger to death, today was different. The dead were different.

The four incoming bodies belonged to terrorists, mass murderers who'd been incarcerated in the ARX Supermax prison two hours north of Bear Claw, and who'd died there under suspicious circumstances. The knowledge that she'd be autopsying their bodies in under an hour gave Chelsea a serious case of the willies as she headed out to meet the prison transport van. No matter how many times she told herself the dead deserved justice, she couldn't talk herself into believing it in this case.

Besides, the bodies came with major political baggage, which meant the ME's office would be under microscopic scrutiny.

Unfortunately, they didn't have a choice in the matter.

Three of the men, who went by the names of al-Jihad, Muhammad Feyd and Lee Mawadi, were international-level terrorists who'd been convicted of the Santa Bombings that had rocked the Bear Claw region three years earlier. The fourth, Jonah Fairfax, had tortured and murdered two federal agents in the days leading up to a bloody government raid on a militant anarchists' compound up in northern Montana, and had apparently hooked up with the terrorists inside the prison, despite being in 24/7 solitary confinement. The four were seriously bad news.

Chelsea, who usually managed to find the upside of any situation, wished the prison had stuck to its standard procedure of handling everything internally, including autopsies. Unfortunately, budget cuts had forced Warden Pollard to pare back his medical staff. When the four prisoners had died of unknown causes within an hour of one another, Pollard had requested an outside autopsy and the state had turfed the bodies to Bear Claw.

"Lucky us," Chelsea muttered as she pushed

through the doors leading to the loading dock, which opened onto a narrow alley separating the two big buildings that housed the ME's office and the main station house of the Bear Claw Creek Police Department.

Two other members of the ME's office were already waiting on the loading ramp: Chelsea's boss and friend, Chief Medical Examiner Sara Whitney, and their newly hired assistant, Jerry Osage. Under normal circumstances there wouldn't have been a welcoming committee for the bodies, but these were far from normal circumstances. The deaths had gained national media attention at a time the ME's office would've strongly preferred otherwise.

That worry was in Sara's eyes as she turned to Chelsea, but her voice held its normal brisk, businesslike tone when she said, "I'm glad you're here. Chief Mendoza wants me to come out front and say a few words for the cameras so we can sneak the van in the back way while the newsies are distracted." Sara slipped out of her fall-weight wool jacket and held it out, revealing a jade-toned skirt suit that perfectly complemented her shoulder-length, honey-colored hair and arresting amber eyes. "Take this in case you're waiting long."

The mid-October day was unusually cool, thanks to a sharp breeze that brought frigid air down from the snow-covered Rockies. It was just another change in the unusually unpredictable weather they'd been having lately. The mix of snow squalls and torrential downpours had triggered landslides in Bear Claw Canyon as well as the hills west of the city, taking out roads and at one point even prompting evacuation of the Bear Claw Ski Resort, which was just starting to gear up for the winter season.

For the moment, though, the skies were clear, the wind sharp. The Rocky Mountains were a dark blur on the horizon, well beyond the huge wilderness of Bear Claw Canyon State Park, which formed an unpopulated buffer between the city suburbs and the ARX Supermax prison.

Chelsea shivered involuntarily, though she couldn't have said whether the chill came from the wind biting through the thin scrubs she wore over her casual slacks and shirt, or the thought of how little actually separated them from an enclosure housing two thousand or so of the worst criminals in the country.

She took Sara's coat and drew it over her shoulders. "Thanks."

The garment was too long everywhere and she didn't have a prayer of buttoning it across the front, mute testimony that Sara was tall and lean and willowy, whereas Chelsea was none of those things.

Five-five if she stretched it, tending way more toward curvy than willowy, Chelsea wore her dark, chestnut-highlighted hair in a sassy bob that brushed her chin, used a daily layer of mascara to emphasize the long eyelashes that framed her brown eyes, and considered her smile to be her best feature. If life were a movie, she would probably play the best friend's supporting role to Sara's elegant lead, and that was okay with her.

Some people were destined to do great things, others small ones. That was just the way it was.

Within the ME's office, Chelsea was good at the small things. She was the best of them at dealing with the families of the dead, mainly because she genuinely liked people. She enjoyed meeting them and learning about them, and she liked knowing that the information she gave them often helped ease the passing of their loved ones. She might not be saving the world, but she was, she hoped, making the natural process of death a bit easier, one family at a time.

At the moment, though, she didn't particularly care if the incoming bodies were tied to people who had loved them and wanted answers. As far as she was concerned, monsters like the four dead men didn't deserve autopsies or answers. They deserved deep, unmarked graves and justice in the afterlife.

"I wish the prison had kept the bodies," Sara grumbled, her thoughts paralleling Chelsea's. Then she sighed, clearly not looking forward to the impromptu press conference. "Okay, I'll go do the song and dance and leave you guys to the real work."

The snippiness implied by her words was more self-directed than anything—as the youngest chief medical examiner in city history, and a woman to boot, she'd found herself doing far more politicking and crisis management than she'd expected, when Chelsea knew she'd rather be in the morgue, doing the work she'd trained for.

The two women had only met the year before, when Sara had pulled Chelsea's résumé out of a stack of better-qualified applicants because she'd been looking to build a young, cutting-edge team that combined empathy with hard science and innovation. That had been great until six months later, when the young, aggressive mayor who'd recruited Sara had stepped down in the wake of an embezzlement scandal, and his old-guard deputy mayor had taken over and promptly started undoing a large chunk of his predecessor's work.

Acting Mayor Proudfoot hadn't yet managed to disassemble the ME's office, but he was trying. That had Sara, Chelsea and the others watching their backs at every turn these days.

"We've got this," Chelsea assured her boss. "You go make us look good, okay?"

Sara shot her a grateful smile and headed inside. When the door shut at her back, Chelsea glanced at Jerry. She grinned at the sight of the assistant's obvious discomfort in the sharp air. "Dude, your nose is turning blue."

Dark-haired and brown-eyed, the twenty-something Florida native was having a tough time adjusting to his first cold snap, having moved to Bear Claw just that summer to be with his park-ranger girlfriend. But Jerry was a hard worker and an asset to the team. He didn't accept her invitation to bitch about the cold, instead saying, "The van's late. Wonder if the driver got lost or stuck in the media circus or something."

Chelsea pulled out her cell and checked the time display, frowning when she saw that he was right, the transpo coming from the prison was a good fifteen minutes overdue. "Maybe I should call the prison dispatcher and see if there's been a delay."

"Never mind. I think I see them."

Sure enough, a plain-looking van nosed its way into the alley, then spun away from them and started backing toward the cement loading dock, its brake lights flashing as the driver struggled to navigate the tight, unfamiliar alley, which was made even tighter by an obstacle course of trash bins and parked vehicles.

Unmarked and unremarkable, the van looked like nothing special on first glance, but a closer inspection revealed that it was reinforced throughout, with mesh on the small back windows.

Through the mesh, Chelsea could see one of the guards' faces. His eyes were a clear, piercing blue, and a thin scar ran through one of his dark eyebrows, probably tangible evidence of the dangers that came from working within the ARX Supermax.

As the van's rear bumper kissed the rubber-padded lip of the dock, the guard's eyes locked on Chelsea and another shiver tried to work its way through her. This one didn't come from the cold or unease about the prisoners' bodies, though; it was a sensual tremor, one that tempted her to rethink the "career first" vow she'd made in the wake of yet another near-miss of a relationship.

The guard's eyes hadn't changed and he hadn't moved, but suddenly her breath came thin in her lungs and she had to lock her legs against a wash of heat and weakness, and an almost overwhelming urge to see the rest of him. In private.

"Wow," she said aloud. "Note to self: take Sara up on her offer to bring her brother around for a look-see." Chelsea might've sworn off serious relationships, but there was no doubt her body was telling her that it was time for some recreational dating.

"'Scuse me?" asked Jerry, who looked confused.

"Just talking to myself," Chelsea said as the van came to a stop and the guard disappeared from the window. She felt a little spurt of disappointment to have their shared look broken off, followed by a kick of nerves that she'd see the rest of him in a moment. Not that she was likely to follow up on the attraction, if it was even reciprocated. His direct, challenging stare warned that he'd probably be too intense for her, too unnerving.

She liked her guys the same way she preferred her Tex-Mex and curry: a little on the mild side, satisfying yet undemanding. She might be drawn to the other kind of guy, the tough, challenging sort she liked in her books and movies, but that was where her inner wimp kicked in. She didn't want to date a guy she couldn't keep up with.

And that was so not what she was supposed to be focusing on right now, she lectured herself as the driver killed the engine and emerged from the vehicle, carrying the requisite paperwork. Moments later, the back doors swung open and two other guys jumped down and started readying the body bags for transfer into the morgue. The men were wearing drab uniforms with weapon belts, and hats pulled low over their brows, making them blend into a certain sort of sameness...except for the blue-eyed guard, who Chelsea recognized immediately, even from the back.

He was maybe five-ten or so, with wide shoulders and ropy muscles that strained the fabric of his uniform, as though he'd bulked up recently and hadn't yet replaced his clothes. His hips were narrow, his legs powerful, and though she'd never really gone for the uniform look before—she was surrounded by cops on a daily basis, so there wasn't much novelty in it—the dark material of his pants did seriously interesting things to his backside when he bent over and fiddled with one of the gurneys, unlocking it from the fasteners that had kept it in place during transport.

As far as she could tell, two of the bodies were on gurneys, two on the floor of the van. Normally she would've been annoyed by the lack of respect for the dead. Not this time, though.

When the driver moved to hand the paperwork to Jerry, the assistant waved it off and pointed at Chelsea. "She's in charge. I'm just the muscle."

She tore herself away from ogling the guard to reach for the clipboard. "I'll take the paperwork. Jerry can help you unload and show you where the bodies go."

The driver frowned. "I thought a guy was supposed to sign off on the delivery. Rickey Charles."

Chelsea flipped through the pages, nodding when everything looked good. Once all the bags were inside the morgue, she would open them up and inspect the bodies, making sure the info matched. Then, and only then, would she sign the papers indicating that she'd accepted the delivery, freeing the guards to make the return trip to the prison.

Not paying full attention to the driver, she said, "Rickey got held up this morning. I'm covering."

Actually, her fellow medical examiner was in lockup, sleeping it off after being arrested on his third DUI, but she wasn't about to advertise the fact. Sara had made a monumental mistake hiring the charismatic young pathologist in the first place, but he was related to one of her higher-ups, and he'd fit the "young and innovative" stamp she'd been trying to put on the ME's office, so she'd given him a chance despite his less-than-stellar recommendations.

That'd come back to bite Sara, but Chelsea knew her friend would handle it quietly. There was no need to gossip.

Noticing that the driver had started to fidget,

she said, "Don't stress. It'll just take a few minutes."

He mumbled something, grabbed the clipboard and turned away, heading back for the van.

"Hey!" she called, starting after him. "I haven't signed off yet."

Just then, Jerry started pushing the first gurney toward the morgue, and she saw that he'd acquired a smear of red on the front of his scrubs.

"Jerry, stop," Chelsea said quickly as a twist of worry locked in her stomach. She crossed to the blue-eyed guard, who was facing away from her, prepping the second bag for transport. She tapped him on the shoulder. "Weren't these body bags surface-cleaned back at the prison?"

They certainly should've been. Not only was it standard protocol, but it was also doubly important in this case, given that they didn't yet know why or how the prisoners had died.

Her guard turned—that was how she found herself thinking of him, as "her guard," though that was silly—and she got the full-on gut punch of his charisma. His features were lean, his skin drawn and pale, and he didn't look like he smiled much. And those eyes…up close they were even more magnetic than she'd thought them from afar, ice blue and arresting, and holding a level of intensity that reached inside her and grabbed on, kindling a curl of heat in her belly.

He looked more like a grown-up than most of the thirty-somethings she knew. He looked like a leader, like someone who would take charge of any situation.

"We're just the transporters," he said, his voice a rough rasp that slid along her nerve endings and left tiny shivers behind. "We're running late, so it'd be best if you signed off on the delivery so we can be on our way." Something moved in his expression, there and gone so quickly she almost missed it, but leaving the impression that his words were more an order than a suggestion.

Nerves fired through her, warning that something wasn't right.

Not liking the feeling, or the strange effect the guard had on her, Chelsea backpedaled a step. But she stuck to operating procedures, saying, "I'm not signing anything if there's blood on the bags. You have no idea what killed these men. For all we know, it could be an infectious agent." She gestured for Jerry to step away from the gurney, and reached for her cell phone. "Leave everything right where it is. I'm calling my boss."

This is so not what Sara needs right now, she thought, but protocol was protocol, and if the medical staff at the ARX Supermax had been so sloppy as to allow the bodies to be shipped without the bags being disinfected first, who knew what other safety precaution they might've skipped?

"Wait," the blue-eyed guard said, holding up a hand. At that same moment, the guard behind him spun and grabbed for something on his belt. A gun.

Chelsea's eyes locked on the weapon, and she froze.

Jerry's head jerked up and his mouth went slack, his eyes locking on the other guard. "Hey, aren't you—"

The man shot him where he stood.

Jerry jerked spasmodically as blood bloomed in the center of his forehead. Then he went limp and fell, his eyes glazing as he dropped, his mouth open in an "O" of surprise.

To Chelsea, the world seemed to slow down, his body collapsing at half-speed. She sucked in a breath to scream, but before she could make a sound, something slammed into her temple, dazing her.

She staggered, only just beginning to realize that the guards weren't guards at all. They were convicts wearing the clothing of the guards who were no doubt filling the body bags in the van. Somehow the prisoners had played dead and then pulled a switch en route.

Heart drumming as her consciousness dimmed, Chelsea fumbled for her phone, and watched it spin out of her grasp and clatter to the ground, which pitched and heaved beneath her. The blue-eyed guard caught her as she fell, supporting her in his strong, steady arms, in a grip that shouldn't have felt as good as it did.

The last thing she comprehended before she passed out was a piercing sense of disappointment that somehow existed alongside the terror. Of course he was trouble; she'd never been truly attracted to any other kind of man. Sara had even joked one time that Chelsea's taste in men was going to be the death of her.

What if she'd been right?

Chapter Two

Jonah Fairfax hadn't touched a woman in nearly nine months, and this was *not* how he'd pictured ending the drought.

When Fax had imagined his reintroduction to feminine companionship from the sterile gloom of his six-by-ten cell, he'd figured on candlelight, good food and soft music, and either a paid escort or a sympathetic friend of a friend. Or, hell, even his handler and sometimes lover, who called herself Jane Doe even in bed.

The woman's identity hadn't been particularly important to his sexual fantasy. What had mattered were the trappings of civilization, the colors and smells, and the textures of real life.

However, that fantasy most definitely hadn't involved a prison meat wagon backed up to the morgue where they'd been stood up by Rickey Charles, the contact who was the key to the next stage in their getaway. And it definitely hadn't starred a pistol-whipped woman hanging limply in his arms…and three seriously nasty terrorists glaring at him like they already regretted involving him in their jailbreak.

Not that they'd had a choice. He'd made damn sure of that, with help from Jane and some of the other agents working underneath her. She headed up a national security agency so secret it didn't even have a name, one that was organized along the lines of the very terror networks it hunted, with each agent functioning as a separate cell, not knowing who else might be involved, or how.

For this particular op, Jane had gotten Fax arrested for murder, constructing such a deep, seamless cover that even his mother and brothers had written him off. That had been the only way to make him useful to al-Jihad, just as orchestrating an escape had been the only way they could come up with to flush out the high-level terrorist's suspected contacts within Homeland Security itself.

The deaths of the prison guards and the morgue attendant were regrettable, but Jane had chosen Fax for the op because she knew he could function in the bloodiest situations and deal with an acceptable level of collateral damage—and innocent lives lost—if it meant getting the job done. It was cold, yes, but necessary.

Jane had honed that level of detachment, perhaps, but he could thank his wife, Abby, for setting him on the path. She'd been dead five years now, and he thought she would've hated what he'd become. No way she would've accepted the part her betrayal had played—she'd never been big on personal accountability. But even as he thought that, Fax was mildly surprised to realize it'd been some time since he'd last thought of the woman who'd been his high-school sweetheart, and later his wife. In the past, her memory had driven him, haunted him, made him into the bloodless man he'd become, the one Jane had needed and wanted.

Now, it seemed, even the warmth of anger was fading, leaving him colder still.

"You gonna kill the bitch or dance with her first?" Lee Mawadi asked, nodding to the woman in Fax's arms with a sneer.

Then again, Lee seemed to do pretty much everything with a sneer. Fax was pretty sure it covered some major insecurities.

Fax didn't know any of his fellow escapees well, because the 24/7 solitary confinement at the ARX Supermax tended to cut down on social discourse. He'd met the three terrorists in person for the first time just an hour earlier, when they'd awoken from the drugs Jane had smuggled to him, which had mimicked death close enough to pass inspection for twelve hours.

Almost immediately upon awakening, Fax had pegged the thirtysomething, blond Lee Mawadi as a wannabe, a follower. Lee had grown up a rich, pampered American, but had developed a love of violence along the way, a desire to kill, and be part of a killing squad. He'd hooked up with al-Jihad and had found the leader he'd been seeking. He'd played the part of a businessman, married a photographer and lived the American dream, all while working as a member of al-Jihad's crew, following orders without question.

Lee was a lemming, but Fax suspected he was a nasty critter, the sort that would bite you before it ran off the cliff in pursuit of its leader.

"No need to kill her," Fax said in answer to Lee's question. "She's out cold." He shifted the woman's deadweight, figuring on dumping her off to the side, out of harm's way. The younger, male morgue attendant was beyond help, but if Fax played it right, he could probably leave the woman alive without attracting too much suspicion. Motioning to the van with his chin, he raised his voice and called to the other members of the small group, "Let's get out of here. Our cover's blown to hell thanks to Lee's itchy trigger finger."

As planned, they'd come out of the coma-inducing meds mid-transpo. Fax had suffered a moment of atavistic terror at finding himself zipped inside a body bag, but al-Jihad had come through as promised. The bag was taped shut rather than zipped, and one of the four guards had distracted the others long enough for the prisoners to emerge from their bags and get into position. Then they'd killed all four guards—including their accomplice, whom al-Jihad didn't trust to stay bought—by breaking their necks, so as to keep their uniforms unbloodied. Then they'd switched places, four for four. Fax didn't know what the death-mimicking meds had contained, but they'd left him with a nasty hangover and occasional double vision. That didn't matter, though. He was still alive, his cover intact. His job was to keep it that way until he figured out who al-Jihad was working with, and what they planned to do next.

With fanatical monsters like him it wasn't a case of if; it was a case of when and where.

"Hey!" Slow to catch the insult, Lee spun in the midst of dragging the younger man's body into the van. "The guy recognized me. I had no choice!"

"Maybe," Fax retorted, propping the woman up against the cold cement wall, partially hidden behind a Dumpster. "Maybe not."

Knowing he was pushing it, he slid a look at the other two men, who as far as he was concerned were far more dangerous than Lee Mawadi.

Muhammad Feyd's dossier pegged the dark-eyed, dark-haired man at thirty-eight, a fanatic among fanatics who'd left al Qaeda in search of a more proactive group of anti-Western terrorists. He'd found exactly that in the man seated in the passenger's seat of the prison transpo van…a man known simply as al-Jihad.

The terrorist leader's dossier was thin, devoid of any information predating the new millennium. He'd appeared on the world stage just before the September 11th terror attacks, had slipped out of the country immediately thereafter, and had played tag with Homeland Security for the next several years. Federal law enforcement suspected that he'd been the mastermind behind numerous bombings and other atrocities, but had never managed to concretely tie him to any of the attacks until he'd finally been tried and convicted for the Santa Bombings that had occurred in several major Colorado cities a few years earlier.

Targeting six shopping malls all owned by the American Mall group, the bombings had been planned to coincide with the ceremonial arrival of the mall Santas to their decorated thrones. All six of the Santas had died…along with the parents and children who'd been lined up, eagerly awaiting the kickoff to the holiday season.

It had been terrorism at its most horrible, and local and federal law enforcement had worked around the clock to indict and convict al-Jihad and his henchmen. They had succeeded, but the evidence had been more circumstantial than proof-positive. The terrorists' high-powered defense attorney had lodged appeal after appeal, but the filings had wound up logjammed in the legal system, which Fax figured was no accident. The courts had no love of terrorists.

The delay had given Jane time to formulate Fax's cover and arrange to have him locked up in the same prison as the terrorist leader and his two lieutenants. She'd turned Fax's honorable military discharge into a dishonorable ousting, cast him in the role of anarchist, invoked the USA PATRIOT Act and held him without trial, making him that much more attractive to an anti-American bastard like al-Jihad.

And thus, an unholy alliance had been born, right on schedule.

In person, the terrorist leader was tall, thin and angular, and graceful enough in his movements that he almost appeared effete…except for his eyes, which were those of a killer.

From reading the available reports, Fax had

known that al-Jihad would be a smart, driven, dangerous man. Meeting him in the flesh had reinforced that impression and added a new realization: the bastard wasn't just dangerous; he was completely without a conscience when it came to killing Americans. Worse, he enjoyed the hell out of it.

That put Fax in an even more tenuous position than he'd anticipated, making it a seriously bad idea to draw attention. Yet that was just what he was risking if he fought too hard to save the pretty medical examiner from becoming part of the collateral damage.

"Boss?" Lee said plaintively, looking at the passenger's seat of the van, where al-Jihad sat silent and square-shouldered.

The terrorist leader sent his follower a dark look that all but said "get a spine," yet he said nothing.

Muhammad aimed a kick at Lee and growled, "Get in the damn van." He jerked his chin at Fax. "You, too. And bring the woman. We'll need a hostage if things get sticky on the way out."

The original plan had been for Rickey Charles—whom al-Jihad had somehow contacted and bribed—to cover the switch for as long as possible, giving them time to get well away. In the absence of that help, their window of opportunity to escape cleanly was closing fast.

"But—" Fax bit off the protest, knowing he was already on tenuous footing with the terrorists.

The only reason he was there at all was because he'd developed the contact for the death-mimicking drugs they'd needed to get on the meat wagon. He'd contacted al-Jihad through a Byzantine trail of notes hidden in the few common areas the prisoners were given access to, one at a time. He'd offered the drug in exchange for a place within al-Jihad's terror cell, and the plan had been born.

Frankly, he was somewhat surprised they hadn't tried to kill him yet, now that they were outside the prison walls. That they hadn't tried to off him indicated that they still had some use for him, but he had a feeling that amnesty wouldn't last long if he started arguing orders.

She's acceptable collateral damage, he told himself, and went back for the woman.

Damned if she didn't stir a little and curl into him when he picked her up and held her against his chest. Surprised, he looked down.

She had dark, chestnut-highlighted hair and faint freckles visible through a fading summer tan. Her cheeks and lips were full, her chin softly rounded, and her nose turned up slightly at the end, giving her an almost childlike, vulnerable air. But there was nothing childlike about the curves that pressed against him, and there was sure as hell nothing juvenile about the unexpected surge of lust that slammed into him when she shifted and turned her face into his neck, so her hair tickled the edge of his ear and feathered across the sensitive skin beneath his jaw.

"Move your ass," Lee snapped from inside the van.

Muhammad finished disabling the vehicle's state-issued GPS locator and got in the driver's seat, then gunned the engine to warn Fax that he was running out of time.

Sometimes it's necessary to sacrifice a few to save the rest, Fax reminded himself. Still, his stomach twisted in a sick ball as he slung the woman through the side door of the vehicle, so she landed near her dead friend, whose corpse was stacked with two of the guards' bodies. The other two bodies were still on the gurneys, one of which was jammed in at an angle where Lee had shoved it in after their escape plan had blown up in their faces.

Even without Rickey Charles, they might've bluffed their way through the body transfer and talked the woman into signing off without confirming the identities of the corpses, but once Lee killed the morgue attendant, even that slim chance had disappeared.

Their escape could get real messy real quick,

Fax knew. Problem was, he needed them to get free so the terrorists would reach out to their contacts and plan their next move.

Which meant the woman's life—and his own, for that matter—were expendable in the grand scheme of things.

Hating the necessity more than he would've expected to, he jumped into the van and rolled the side door closed just as Muhammad hit the gas and the van peeled away from the ME's office.

The four men braced to hear the alarm raised any second, to see pursuit behind them. But there was no alarm, no pursuit as al-Jihad's second in command navigated the city streets of Bear Claw.

Fax noted that they were heading roughly northward, back in the direction of the prison rather than away, but he didn't ask why, didn't even let on that he'd noticed or even cared. He simply filed the information, and hoped like hell he'd have a chance to get it to Jane before al-Jihad and the others decided he'd outlived his usefulness.

Maybe five miles outside the city limits, well down a deserted road that wound through the state forest, Muhammad pulled off into a small parking lot that served a trailhead leading into the wilderness.

Al-Jihad, who was still riding shotgun, turned

to Lee and Fax, and said in his dead, inflection-less voice, "Kill the woman and dump all of the bodies in the canyon. We won't need them where we're going."

Which is where? Fax wanted to ask but didn't because he knew the game too well. The more he followed orders without question, the longer he would live, and the more information he'd gain about the structure of al-Jihad's network inside the U.S.

So instead of asking the questions he wanted answered, he nodded and rolled open the side door, then waited while Lee climbed out. When the other man turned back, Fax shoved one of the body bags at him.

Lee caught the dead guard and nearly went down. "Watch it!" he snapped, glaring at Fax.

"Sorry," Fax said with little remorse, having already figured out that al-Jihad and Muhammad liked the fact that he didn't let the lemming push him around. Jerking his chin in the direction of the trailhead, he said, "I'll be right behind you."

Lee muttered something under his breath, but slung the body bag over his shoulder in a fireman's carry, and headed off into the woods, struggling only slightly under his burden.

Hyperaware of the scrutiny he was receiving from the two men in the front of the van, Fax reached down for the woman, his mind spinning as he desperately tried to figure out a way to keep her alive while protecting his cover.

He didn't know her name, but somehow she'd become the symbol of all the warm, civilized things he'd dreamed of from the confines of his cell, all the beauty and laughter he lived in the darkness to protect.

Jane might be his boss and sometimes lover, but the pretty medical examiner was a real person, one who belonged in the sunlight, not the shadows.

Hefting her over his shoulder, he turned and headed into the forest in Lee's wake. Once he was out of earshot, he said under his breath, "I know you're awake. Don't do anything stupid and you might live to see our backs."

CHELSEA STIFFENED at the sound of his voice, but was too terrified to process his words. The only reason she wasn't already screaming was because she was too damn scared to breathe. That, and she was pretty sure there was nobody nearby to hear except the escaped convicts, who would probably enjoy her terror. So she kept the panic inside, save for the tears that leaked from beneath her screwed-shut eyelids.

She couldn't believe she'd been kidnapped,

couldn't believe that the blue-eyed guard—or rather, the blue-eyed *escaped convict*—she'd been ogling on the loading dock was carrying her into the state forest, acting on a terrorist's orders to kill her and dump her in Bear Claw Canyon.

Things like that just didn't happen to small-scale people like her.

She would've thought it was all a dream, a nightmare, except that the sensations were too real: her head pounded from the blow that'd knocked her unconscious, her tears were cool on her cheeks, and the man's shoulder dug into her belly as he carried her along the path. Opening her eyes, she saw that what she'd figured were signs of recent muscle gain were actually places where his uniform didn't fit; the material gapped at the small of his back, where he'd tucked the guard's weapon into his belt.

WWJBD? She knew she should struggle, she should try to escape, but when? Now or after they reached their destination? What were the chances she could grab that gun and turn the tables?

"Don't," he warned in a low voice.

Before she could respond, or act, or do anything, really, she heard another man's voice from up ahead, saying, "I found a cave. Dump her and put a bullet in her. I'll go get another load."

The man's voice was casual, careless, like he

was talking about things rather than people. But to him she and the others *were* things, she realized. They were Americans. The enemy. Yet the speaker was blond, and his voice carried a trace of a Boston accent. She would've passed him on the street and never once thought to wonder about him.

Vaguely, she remembered a snippet of newscast that'd said one of the three escapees, Lee Mawadi, was a homegrown terrorist who'd hooked up with al-Jihad for the Santa Bombings.

Back then, sitting safe in her living room, terrorism had been an abstract concept, something she saw on TV and exclaimed over while secretly thinking that such things would never happen to her. She hadn't even been in Colorado during the Santa Bombings; she'd been finishing a nice, safe rotation in a private practice outside Chicago, reveling in the early stages of a relationship she'd thought was The One, but had turned out to be another Not Quite.

Now, though, she was all alone, with terror her only companion.

"Sounds good to me," the man carrying her said, his voice easy as he agreed to the plan of shooting her and dumping her in the cave.

But his touch, while firm, was disconcertingly gentle and he'd hinted at the possibility that she might live. Did that mean he had a soft spot for her because of their shared look out by the loading dock? Would he somehow prove to be an ally?

Get a grip, her inner voice of practicality snapped. *He's a murderer.*

If the other speaker was Lee Mawadi, then the blue-eyed man she'd shared a long look with must be Jonah Fairfax. That meant he hadn't been part of the Santa Bombings, but it didn't make him innocent or safe. The ARX Supermax didn't cater to white-collar criminals, and Fairfax had been jailed for torturing and murdering two of the FBI agents sent to infiltrate the anarchist camp he'd been a member of.

Yet he'd made it sound like he wanted to save her somehow. It made no sense.

When footsteps warned that the other man— Lee Mawadi—was passing them on the trail, Chelsea screwed her eyes shut. Moments later, the sunlight beyond her eyelids cut to black and the echoes told her that they'd entered the cave he'd spoken of.

The blue-eyed man—Fairfax—flipped her off his shoulder without warning, then caught her before she could slam to the ground. She kept her eyes shut as he lowered her so she was half propped up against a rock wall. She could feel him crouch over her, leaning close and blocking any hope of escape.

"I need you to stop playing dead and listen very carefully," he said, his voice low and urgent. "I think I can get you out of this, but you're going to have to trust me."

She opened her eyes at that, and nearly screamed when she saw that he'd put her down right next to one of the body bags. Worse, it was open, revealing one of the dead guards, shirtless, his eyes open and staring in death.

She held in the scream, but plastered herself against the rock wall, her quick, panicked breaths rattling in her lungs.

"Look at me." The blue-eyed man touched her chin and turned her head toward him. "Don't scream and don't move. Lee is going to be back in a minute, so we've got to work fast." He paused as though gauging her. "I need to get something out of my shoe. Can I trust you not to try to run?"

She nodded quickly, though she didn't mean it. The second an opportunity presented, she was so out of there.

He gave her another, longer look. "Yeah. That's what I thought." As though he'd read her mind, he stayed between her and the mouth of the cave, which was little more than a crevice in the rock, probably part of the canyon that'd been pushed up and over ground level by a long-ago glacier or earth shift, or maybe even one of the recent landslides.

Fairfax worked at his right shoe for a moment and came up with a small ampoule of pale yellow liquid. He crowded close to her, leaving no room for retreat or escape. "This is going to knock you out and depress your vitals so far that it'll look like you're dead, but you won't be. You'll come around in twelve hours or so, and we'll be long gone."

Then, before she could react, before she could protest, or scream, or any of the other things she knew she damn well ought to do, he'd broken off the tip of the ampoule, jammed the needle-point end into her upper arm, and squeezed the yellow liquid into her.

Pain flared at the injection site, hard and hot.

She opened her mouth to scream but nothing came out. She struggled to stand up and run, but her legs wouldn't obey. Her muscles turned to gelatin and she started sliding sideways, and this time Fairfax didn't catch her or break her fall.

She heard him stand, heard a weapon's action being racked in preparation for firing. Then there was a single gunshot.

Then nothing.

FAX KNEW HE didn't have much time, if any. He went to his knees beside the body bag containing the dead guard, whom he'd just shot. Pressing his hand against the wound, he got as much cool blood as he could from the dead man, and slathered it across the unconscious woman's face, concentrating on the hair above her temple.

When he heard footsteps at the entrance to the cave, he readjusted the body bag and wiped off his hands on part of the woman's coat, then tucked the stained section beneath her before he stood.

Feigning nonchalance, he put the safety on his gun and stuck the weapon in his waistband before he turned toward Lee, hoping like hell the lemming wouldn't notice that the blood on the woman wasn't exactly fresh.

Only the newcomer wasn't Lee. It was al-Jihad himself.

The terrorist leader stood silhouetted at the cave mouth, a lean, dark figure whose presence was significantly larger than his physical self.

A shiver tried to crawl down the back of Fax's neck but he held it off, determined to brazen out the situation and keep himself in the killer's good graces. Gesturing casually toward the woman, he said, "She's all set. Want me to go help Lee with the other guards?"

Al-Jihad moved past him without a word, gliding almost silently, seeming incorporeal, like the demon he was. Crouching down beside the woman's motionless, blood-spattered body, he touched her cheek, then her throat, checking for a pulse.

Fax forced himself not to tense up, reminded himself to breathe, to act like the cold, jaded killer Abby's betrayal had made him into. Only the thing was, something had changed inside him. He'd been playing the role of convict for so long it'd become second nature to hold the persona within the prison, but he found he was in danger of slipping now that they were outside those too-familiar walls.

Hell, face it; he'd already slipped. There was no rational reason for him to jeopardize his position by faking the woman's murder. The ampoule of the death-mimicking meds he'd tucked into a false, X-ray-safe compartment inside one of his not-quite-prison-issue shoes was supposed to be a safety net, a way for him to fake his own death if the need arose. Similarly, the GPS homing device he'd activated and placed in her coat pocket was supposed to be used only if he thought he was in imminent danger of being killed, and wanted to make sure Jane could find his body.

Sure, he'd also planted a message on the woman, information he needed to get to Jane. But he could've gotten the info to her in other ways, ones that wouldn't have used up so much of his dwindling bag of tricks.

So why had he gone all out to save a woman whose name he knew only because he'd palmed the ID tag off her scrubs?

Reaching into his pocket to touch the plastic tag, which read *Chelsea Swan*—a lovely name for a lovely woman—he thought he knew why he'd endangered himself and his mission for her. It was the freckles. Abby had had freckles like that, back when they'd been high-school sweethearts, before he'd done his stint in the military, blithely assuming things would stay the same while he was gone.

Back when Abby'd had freckles, their biggest problems had been arguments over which movie to see, or which radio station to play as they'd tooled around town in his beat-up Wrangler with the soft top down. Eventually, though, she'd outgrown her freckles…and him.

Chelsea Swan reminded him of those earlier times. Good times. Times that might as well have happened to someone else. But because they hadn't, and because she looked like the sort of person who ought to have more good times ahead of her, he'd dabbed blood over her scalp and face to simulate a head wound, and he'd used his meds to make her body play dead.

Question was, would it be enough to save her?

Al-Jihad stood without a word, and gestured for Fax to return to the vehicle. "Go help Lee."

Fax stayed tense as he followed orders, fearing that al-Jihad was playing him, that the bastard knew what he'd done and was teasing him with the illusion of success. But the terrorist leader returned to the van a few minutes later, and on Fax's next trip into the cave, he saw that Chelsea remained just as he'd left her.

He and Lee finished unloading the other bodies, opening up each of the bags so the scent would attract scavengers, in hopes that they'd deface the bodies, further complicating forensic analysis when the dump site was eventually found. At least that was the terrorists' theory. In reality, the homing beacon would have Jane's people on-site in a few hours.

Once the job was done, Fax hung back in the cave.

"Move it," Lee snapped when they both heard an impatient horn beep from the direction of the road. "The cops'll get the roadblocks up soon."

"I'm right behind you," Fax said. But as the other man hustled down the trail, Fax stayed put.

Moving fast, he pulled the jacket and heavy sweatshirt off the dead morgue attendant, and packed them around Chelsea's limp body. When that didn't look like it'd be enough, he whispered,

"Sorry," and pulled the attendant's still-warm corpse over her as added insulation. It was too cold and her vitals were too depressed for him to worry about niceties. If Jane took too long to respond, Chelsea could freeze to death.

Hopefully, though, Jane would send someone right away. The responding agent could then administer the counteragent to the death-mimicking drug, collect the GPS beacon and info pellet Fax had planted on Chelsea, and phone in an untraceable tip that would lead the locals to the location. The agent would undoubtedly also reset the scene, making it look as though her survival had been accidental rather than intentional.

With no way of knowing where al-Jihad had eyes and ears, they had to be careful not to make it obvious that the terrorist had a traitor among his small crew.

"Just hang on for a few hours, Chelsea," Fax said quietly, his words echoing in the cave. "Help should be on its way soon."

Then, knowing he'd done the best he could for her, he paused at the cave mouth and looked back at the six bloodied bodies, five of which weren't going to wake up ever again.

"Collateral damage," he murmured. Uncharacteristically, he found himself regretting that he couldn't have saved the others, hadn't even tried.

And, as he walked into the sunlight, he found himself wishing that he believed he was going to live long enough to see pretty Chelsea Swan again, under better circumstances.

But as soon as he caught himself thinking along those lines, he squelched the emotions.

There was no room for softness around men like al-Jihad, and Fax had a job to do. That took priority, period.

Chapter Three

"She's coming around." Chelsea felt a couple of light taps on her face, and heard a babble of voices close by, but she couldn't quite grasp what any of it meant.

Reality and recognition were distant strangers. Cocooned in a warm lassitude, she felt too lazy to move, too tired to care that moving was impossible.

"Are you sure none of this is her blood?" a second voice asked, this one female.

"Positive," the first voice answered. "She doesn't have a single laceration on her, just the bump on the back of her head."

"Then where'd the blood come from?"

"From one of the others, looks like." Another series of taps on her face. "Chelsea? Can you hear me?"

She moaned and swatted at the hand that was gently slapping her. At least she tried to swat. She failed, though, because her arms didn't move.

"Here she comes," the first voice said, sounding pleased. "Okay, kiddo. I need you to open your eyes now. Can you do that for me?"

Chelsea did as she was told, squinting into the fading light of dusk, which showed that she was inside a cave of sorts. The details were lost to the shadows and the glare of handheld lights, but she was aware of numerous people inside the small space, most of them cops.

A paramedic was crouched over her. Behind a plastic face shield, his brown eyes were dark with concern. It wasn't the concern that confused her though; it was her sudden, utter conviction that his eyes were the wrong color. They weren't supposed to be brown; they were supposed to be...

Blue, she remembered. Ice-cold blue.

The memory of the man's eyes unlocked a flood of other recollections. She gasped as the memories swamped her, slapping her with terror and confusion, and the unbelievable realization that Jonah Fairfax, double murderer, had done exactly as he'd promised. He'd saved her.

But as the pieces lined up in her brain—sort of— they didn't click. He'd said the drug would take twelve hours to wear off, and she'd been abducted near lunchtime, yet she could see dusk outside.

"What day is it?" she asked, her voice cracking

from disuse and whatever drug he'd stuck in her system.

The paramedic said, "Tuesday. Why?"

Which meant she'd only been out for a few hours. "How did you find me?"

"Anonymous tip," he said, looking past her to confer with someone outside her line of vision.

Her brain jammed on the information, which didn't make sense. Fairfax had said something about the escapees being well away by the time she came around, but she'd only been out for a few hours. Had he changed his mind and made the call himself? Had—

The spiraling questions bounced off each other inside her throbbing skull and logjammed, and a sudden shiver wracked her body. "I'm f-freezing," she managed between chattering teeth.

"We're working on that," the paramedic replied. "We'll have you out of here in a jiff."

It wasn't until he and his partner lifted her that she realized she was on a stretcher, swathed in blankets and strapped down, which explained the feeling of immobility.

She was aware of commotion around her as she was carried out of the cave and back along the wooded trail. She caught glimpses of concerned faces, many of them belonging to cops she saw in the ME's office on a regular basis. She wanted to stop and talk to them, wanted to tell them what had happened to her, but her lips didn't work right and the light was all funny, going from the blue of dusk to a strange grayish-brown and back again.

When they reached the ambulance, Sara was there waiting, tears coursing down her cheeks when she saw Chelsea. Her lips moved; the words didn't make any sense but Chelsea knew her friend well enough to guess Sara was apologizing for leaving her out on the loading dock.

It wasn't your fault, Chelsea tried to say. *Don't blame yourself. I'll be okay—Fairfax saved me.* But the words didn't come out. She couldn't move, couldn't speak, couldn't do anything but let the world slip away as the paramedics loaded her into the waiting ambulance.

Everything faded to the gray-brown of unconsciousness.

She surfaced a few times after that—once as she was being wheeled through the hospital corridors, the fluorescent lights flashing brightly overhead, and once again during some sort of exam, when she heard doctors' and nurses' voices saying things like, "That doesn't make any sense" and "Check it again."

She didn't come around fully until early the next morning. She knew it was morning because of the way the light of dawn bled pale lavender through the slatted blinds that covered the room's single window, and the way her body was suddenly clamoring for breakfast and coffee, not necessarily in that order.

A quick look around confirmed that she was, indeed, in the hospital, and added the information that homicide detective Tucker McDermott was fast asleep in the chair beside her bed.

The realization warmed her with the knowledge that her friends had closed ranks around her already.

She knew Tucker through the ME's office, and more importantly through his wife, Alyssa, who was a good friend. Alyssa, a forensics specialist within the BCCPD, was quick-tempered and always on the go. In contrast, Tucker was a rock, steady and dependable. He might've had a flighty playboy's reputation a few years back, but marriage had settled him to the point that he'd become the go-to guy in their circle, the one who was always level in a crisis, always ready to listen or offer a shoulder to lean on.

He made her wimpy side feel safe.

She must've moved or made some sound indicating that she'd awakened, because he opened his eyes, blinked a couple of times, then smiled. "Hey. How are you feeling?"

"I'm—" She paused, confused. "That's weird. I feel fine. Better than fine, actually. I feel really good." Energy coursed through her alongside the gnawing hunger, but there were none of the lingering aches she would've expected from her ordeal. Lifting a hand, which didn't bear an IV or any monitoring lines, she probed the back of her head and found a bruised lump, but little residual pain. Oddly, though, she didn't feel the brain fuzz of prescription-strength painkillers. "What did the doctors give me?"

Tucker shook his head. "Nothing. By the time you arrived, your core temp was coming back up and your vitals were stabilizing. They decided to let you sleep it off and see how you felt when you woke up."

"I'm okay," she said weakly, her brain churning. "Okay" wasn't entirely accurate, though, because the more she thought about her ordeal the more scared and confused she became, as terrifying images mixed with the memory of the convict who'd saved her life, and the coworker who'd lost his.

"Jerry's dead, isn't he?" she asked softly.

She remembered the gunshot, remembered him falling, even remembered him lying in the van, limp in death, but a piece of her didn't want to accept that he was gone. She wanted to believe he'd been stunned like she'd been. Not dead. Not Jerry, with his cold nose and ski-bunny girlfriend.

But Tucker shook his head, expression full of remorse. "I'm sorry."

Chelsea closed her eyes, grief beating at her alongside guilt. She should've done something different. If she hadn't been staring at Fairfax, she might've been quicker to recognize that there was a problem with the delivery. She might've been able to—

"Don't," Tucker said. "You'll only make yourself crazy trying to 'what if' this. If you'd done something different, they probably would've killed you, too."

"They did, sort of," Chelsea whispered, her breath burning her throat with unshed tears.

Tucker shifted, pulled out his handheld, which acted as both computer and cell phone. "You okay if I record this?"

She nodded. "Of course." No doubt she'd have to go through her statement over and over again with a variety of cops and agents, but this first time she'd rather talk to Tucker than anyone else.

Haltingly at first, she told him what had happened, her words coming easier once she got started, then flowing torrentlike when she described waking up in the van and realizing she'd been kidnapped by the escapees, followed by

Fairfax's strange actions. She kept it facts only, reporting what he'd done and said, and figuring she'd leave it to Tucker and the others to draw their own conclusions.

When she was done, she glanced at Tucker and was unsurprised to see a concerned frown on his face.

"That sounds…"

"Bizarre," she filled in for him. "Like something from a not-very-believable action movie. I know. But that's what happened."

He nodded, but she could tell he didn't believe her. Or rather, he probably believed that *she* believed what she was saying, but thought her so-called memories were more along the lines of drug-induced hallucinations shaped by her penchant for spy movies that always included at least one double agent and a couple of twists.

Then again, she thought with a start, what if he was right? She felt terrible that she'd been paying more attention to Fairfax's butt than to her job and the potential security risks, opening the way for Jerry's murder. What if her subconscious had taken that guilt and woven a fantasy that cast the object of her attraction as a hero, making her lapse, if not acceptable, then at least less reprehensible?

"Maybe I'm not remembering correctly," she said after a moment.

"The info about Rickey Charles fits," Tucker said, though he still sounded pretty dubious. "He was found dead in his holding cell this morning."

Chelsea sat up so fast her head spun. "He what?"

Tucker winced. "I should've phrased that better. Sorry, I went into cop-talking-to-ME mode and forgot you knew him."

"What did he—" Chelsea broke off, not sure how she was supposed to feel. She hadn't cared for Rickey and couldn't forgive that he'd apparently made some sort of deal with the escapees, but she wouldn't have wished him dead under any circumstance.

"It was murder concocted to look like a suicide," Tucker said succinctly. "I guess, based on what you just told me about what the driver said to you out on the loading dock, that Rickey was supposed to have signed off on the bodies, delaying discovery of the switch. When he turned up in the holding cell instead, someone working for al-Jihad killed him either to punish him or to shut him up, or both."

Which would mean that someone in the PD—or at least someone with access to the overnight holding cells—was on the terrorists' payroll, Chelsea thought. She didn't say it aloud, though, because the possibility was too awful to speak.

Tucker nodded, though. "Yeah. Big problem. That's why I'm here."

He hadn't stayed with her strictly to keep her company, she realized. He'd stayed because the BCCPD had figured it might not be a coincidence that the ME who'd missed his shift that morning had wound up dead. Tucker's bosses—and her own—thought she might be at risk, that whoever had killed Rickey might go after her next, looking to silence her before she told the cops anything that might help lead them to the escapees.

Except she didn't know anything that would help, did she?

"Don't worry," Tucker said, correctly interpreting her fears. "We're keeping the story as quiet as possible, and letting the media think you're dead, too. If the escapees are following the news, they have no reason to think you're alive."

Unless Fairfax had told them for some reason. But why would he, when he'd been the one to save her?

She didn't know who to trust, or what to believe, and the confusion made her head spin.

She sank back against the thin hospital pillow, noticing for the first time that she was wearing nothing but a hospital johnnie and a layer of bedclothes. "Can I—" she faltered as the world she knew seemed to skew beneath her, tilting precariously. "Can I get dressed and get out of here?"

His expression went sympathetic. "Yeah, you're

cleared…medically, anyway. Since your purse was still at the office, Sara used your key to grab clothes, shoes and a jacket for you, along with a few toiletries." He gestured. "They're in the bathroom, along with your purse. The keys are in it."

He didn't offer to help her, which told her it was a test: if she couldn't make it to the bathroom and get herself dressed unassisted, she was staying in the hospital until she could.

She'd been telling the truth, though. She felt fantastic—physically, anyway—and was able to make it to the small restroom and get dressed without any trouble.

In the midst of pulling on her shirt, she paused and frowned in confusion when she saw that there wasn't any discernible mark where the injection had gone into her arm. He'd jammed the tip of that ampoule in hard enough that it should've left a mark. Did that mean it hadn't happened the way she remembered?

It didn't take too many minutes of staring at her own reflection in the mirror for her to conclude that she didn't know, and she wasn't going to figure it out standing in a hospital bathroom. She emerged to find Tucker waiting for her, with his cell phone pressed to his ear.

"You shouldn't be on that thing in here," she said automatically, her med-school training kicking in even though the actual risk was relatively minor.

"I'm off," he said, flipping the phone shut and dropping it in his pocket. "You ready to go?" He indicated the door with a sweep of his hand.

He didn't offer to let her in on the phone call that'd been so important he'd broken hospital rules to take it, but his eyes suggested it was something about her, or the escapees.

Have you caught them? she wanted to ask, but didn't because she feared it would come out sounding as though she hoped the men were still at large. Not that she did—her terrifying ordeal had more than convinced her that al-Jihad, Muhammad Feyd and Lee Mawadi were monsters who didn't even deserve the benefit of an autopsy.

"The man who helped me, or who I think helped me, anyway…that was Jonah Fairfax, right?" she couldn't help asking.

She hadn't wanted to say too much about him, lest Tucker read too much into her words. But it wasn't like she was going to be able to ask anyone else either.

After a long moment, he inclined his head. "Yeah. The description fits."

"Have they been caught yet?"

"No." Tucker paused. "Maybe it'd be better for

you to stay in the hospital a little longer, for observation."

Translation: I think you should go upstairs to the psych ward and have a nice chat with a professional about the definition of Stockholm syndrome.

"That's not necessary," she said quickly. "I'm feeling fine. Hungry, but otherwise fine."

"Are you sure?"

"Don't worry about me," she said, summoning a smile. "I'm not confused about Fairfax, and I'm ready to do the debriefing thing. I figure I might as well get it over with." She took a deep breath and beat back her nerves. "I promise I'll hold it together."

And she did. She held it together while they returned to the BCCPD by way of a breakfast sandwich to soothe her hunger pangs. Once she was at the PD, she held it together through several more rounds of questioning. The worst of it came from Romo Sampson, a dark-haired, dark-eyed suit from the Internal Affairs Department, but she stayed strong and answered his questions fully on everything except the way her heart had bumped when she first saw Fairfax. That much she kept to herself.

After the questioning, Chelsea also held it together—more or less—through a tearful reunion with Sara and her other coworkers, and a trip down to the morgue to say goodbye to Jerry. She held it together through a phone call to Jerry's devastated girlfriend, and then through calls to her own parents and sister. Each person she spoke to or saw was cautioned to pretend they hadn't heard from her if asked; her survival was being kept very quiet because the escapees—three of them, anyway—thought she was dead. The fourth was still an enigma.

Once she was off the phone with her mother, Chelsea thought about calling her father, but didn't. Despite her mother's best efforts to keep the family together, her parents had divorced when she was in her early teens. Her boat-captain father, a charismatic man with a wandering heart, had called and visited a few times a year for the first few years after the divorce, but that had dwindled and eventually stopped. Last Chelsea had heard, he was living with a woman twenty years his junior, running charters off the Florida Keys. He didn't have a TV, and if he happened to hear about the escape, he probably wouldn't even remember she lived in Bear Claw.

Besides, she figured he'd lost the right to worry about her, in the process teaching her a valuable lesson that had only been reinforced in the years since: men who seemed larger than life usually cared more about that life than they did the people around them.

Chelsea, on the other hand, cared very deeply about her mother and sister, and the friends who had become her extended family in Bear Claw.

Just because she cared, though, didn't mean she was going to let them run her life; she stood her ground when it was time for her to go home, and each of her friends had a different theory on where she should stay, none of the answers being "at home," which was where she wanted to be.

Mindful that Tucker was still watching her for signs of collapse—or Stockholm syndrome—she held it together through the arguments that ensued when she insisted on going home that night, and refused to let any of her friends stay over.

She loved them, she really did, but her self-control was starting to wear seriously thin. She just wanted some alone time, some space to fall apart. Permission to be a wimp.

"Seriously," Sara persisted, "I don't mind."

You might not, but I do, Chelsea thought, her temper starting to fray. She just wanted to go home and cry. "I'll be fine," she said, pulling on her coat. "I'll be under police protection, for heaven's sake." Tucker had arranged to have a patrol car watch from out front of her place, just in case. She shook her head and said, "Honestly, what can you do that the cops can't?" Like her, Sara was an ME. They didn't carry guns, didn't live in the line of fire.

Not usually, anyway.

"I'll listen if you want to talk," Sara said softly, quick hurt flashing in her eyes.

"I'm all talked out," Chelsea said firmly. But she leaned forward and pressed her cheek to Sara's. "I'll call you if that changes, I promise."

She held her spine straight as she marched out of the ME's office, and made herself stay strong as she drove home in her cute little VW Bug, hyperaware of the Crown Vic following close behind her, carrying the surveillance team.

After an uneventful commute, made unusual only by the fact that she couldn't turn on the radio without hearing some mention of the jailbreak and her own supposed death, she pulled her cherry-red Bug into her driveway.

The small, cottagelike house faced a side road and had large-lot neighbors on either side, with a finger of Bear Claw Canyon State Park stretching across her back boundary. The rent was on the high side, but she liked the feeling of space and isolation. At least she usually liked it. Given the events of the day, she wondered whether she might've been better off in a hotel for the night.

No, she decided. She wanted to be in her own space, surrounded by familiar things. Besides, she'd be safe. The cops would see to it.

The Crown Vic pulled in behind her car and

two officers got out; one stayed with her while the other went into the house first and looked around to make sure she was safe and alone.

Wrapping her arms around herself, she waited, shivering slightly even though the car's heater was going full blast. Then again, why shouldn't she shiver? She'd been kidnapped and nearly killed, and had gotten away only by the grace of God and the unexpected help she'd received from the fourth escapee. Or so she thought.

Fairfax was as much of a monster as the others he'd been caged with, Tucker had told her pointedly earlier in the day, and Chelsea knew he was right. She also knew he'd been warning her not to romanticize, as though he'd picked up on the fact that she kept thinking about the man who'd protected her, even though she knew she shouldn't.

Fairfax's angular face was fixed in her mind, and the sound of his voice reverberated in her bones. She couldn't help thinking that if they'd met under different circumstances she would've found him handsome. Heck, even under the current circumstances, she was having serious trouble reconciling the facts with her perception of the man.

Then again, she'd never had very good instincts when it came to guys. Or rather, her instincts were okay; she just tended to ignore them. She'd seen what her mother had gone through with her father. And she'd been through a couple of near-miss relationships that had only reconfirmed that she needed to find herself a guy who might not be all that exciting, but was loyal and relationship-focused.

Yet here she was, practically fantasizing about an escaped double murderer. Maybe she *should* be checking out the hospital's psych ward.

The cop who'd stood guard by her car knocked on the window, making Chelsea jump.

"Sorry," he said when she opened the door, "didn't mean to startle you."

She shook her head. "It's not your fault. I was spacing out." She glanced at the front door, and saw his partner waiting there. "The house is all clear?"

"I'll walk you up." He escorted her to the front door, where he and his partner turned down her offers of coffee, food or a restroom, and then left her to return to their vehicle, where they would spend the night, making regular patrols to ensure that the escapees didn't try to contact her, or worse.

When the cops were gone, Chelsea shut the front door, and locked and deadbolted it for good measure.

Then she turned, leaned back against the panel, and burst into tears.

She'd held it together like she'd promised Tucker she would. Now that she was alone, she gave herself permission to fall apart.

Sinking down until she was sitting on the floor with her spine pressed up against the entryway wall, she cried for Jerry and his girlfriend, and for Rickey, even though he didn't deserve her tears. She cried for the four dead guards laid out in the morgue, two of whom had been a father and son working together. And she cried for herself—for the fear and confusion of being abducted and then rescued by a man she'd been attracted to, a man who'd been called a monster by people she trusted.

Above all, she cried because when it came down to it, she'd frozen. She hadn't struggled or fought, had only survived because of a series of events she didn't understand. She hadn't saved herself. She'd just curled into a little ball and let bad things happen.

It didn't matter what 007 or any of the others would've done. She'd done nothing.

A long time passed before her tears dried up, but eventually they did.

When that happened she swiped her hands across her eyes and drew a deep breath. "You're okay," she told herself. "You're going to be okay."

Thinking things might look a little less grim if she ate something—the breakfast sandwich she'd had seemed aeons in the past—she stood and headed for the kitchen.

She was almost there when a man stepped into the kitchen doorway. She saw his silhouette first, big and muscular, then his dark hair, the lines that cut beside his mouth, and piercing blue eyes that seemed to bore into hers. He was wearing tough-looking black cargo pants and heavy boots, along with a thick sweater and scarred leather jacket, rather than the guard's uniform from before, but she recognized him instantly.

Fairfax.

Heart jolting into her throat, Chelsea screamed. At least she tried to. But he moved too quickly, getting an arm across her collarbones and pressing lightly on her throat while he clapped a hand across her mouth, holding her body motionless as effectively as he trapped the scream in her lungs.

"Don't," he ordered. "I won't hurt you."

Rationality said she should fight, but she hesitated instead, still caught up inside her own skull, torn between attraction and logic, between gratitude and fear.

When she stilled, his grip loosened a fraction. "Good girl," he said, which was patronizing yet somehow soothed her, for reasons she promised herself she'd analyze later. "You going to behave if I let you go?"

She nodded as her pulse hammered in her veins.

"Okay. Here goes." He let his hands fall away, and stepped back.

Chelsea bolted for the front door, screaming, "Help! Help me!"

She heard his bitter curse, heard his footsteps too close behind as she grabbed the knob and twisted. Before she could get the door open, she found herself hanging midair, suspended by her belt and the back of her shirt.

"Damn it." He half hauled, half carried her into the living room, where he tossed her on the sofa. Then he loomed over her, cold blue eyes snapping with temper. "I said I'm not going to hurt you. Settle down!"

She glared back. "Why should I do anything you say?"

"I—" He snapped his jaw shut and exhaled. "Because you owe me one. I saved your life."

Of all the things for her to feel at that moment, disappointment probably wasn't the most logical. But that was what flooded through her, alongside a flare of anger and disillusionment at the realization that he was no different from the others, after all. He hadn't saved her because she'd aroused some soft emotion in him. He'd saved her so he could use her.

"You want me to help you escape," she said, voice flat with anger.

"I managed that one on my own, thanks."

"Then what—" She thought of Rickey's body and shuddered. "You're going to kill me after all."

He shook his head, managing to look both frustrated and vaguely insulted without a change in his cool blue eyes. "No, I'm not going to kill you. I need you to sneak me inside the ME's office."

That confused her enough to dampen some of her panic, especially given that he hadn't made a move in her direction since tossing her on the couch. He was keeping half his attention on the windows—being careful not to cross between them and the light—and the other half on their conversation. He wasn't concentrating on her, wasn't making her feel any immediate menace.

He was treating her like a means to an end, nothing more. Like the way one of her fictional spy heroes would treat an asset.

"Why do you want to break into the ME's office?" she asked, not sure if she'd stopped trying to escape because she was frozen in shock, or if it was because of the way the inexplicable events of the day were realigning themselves in her head, shaping themselves into an impossible hypothesis.

"I need information on Rickey Charles's murder."

Which either meant that Rickey hadn't been

killed on al-Jihad's order…or Fairfax was clandestinely working against the terrorists somehow.

That might explain why he'd been unable to kill her in cold blood, and why he'd had a death-mimicking drug hidden in the heel of his shoe, one that hadn't shown up on any of the tests the doctors had run, and had left her feeling energized rather than half-dead. It was a high-tech, classified drug of some sort, one that—

She stalled her train of thought before it went off the rails, because the scenario was too Hollywood to be real.

Still, she couldn't help asking, "Who…who do you work for?"

Surprise flashed in his eyes, one of the few emotions she'd been able to read there during her brief association with the escaped convict—or whatever he really was.

"The group doesn't have a name," he said carefully.

She felt a spurt of something that shouldn't have seemed like excitement. "Who signs your checks?"

"No checks. I'm paid in wire transfers from shell companies held by other shell companies." But he knew what she was asking, and finally said, "If you go deep enough, the money comes from the U.S. government."

"You're undercover."

He nodded to the bookshelves that lined most of one wall of her living room. They were filled with paperbacks and DVDs. "You read too many spy novels."

"You're telling me I'm wrong?"

"No, just that you shouldn't confuse fiction with reality."

"Did you kill those FBI agents? The ones in Montana?"

He shook his head. "No. That was part of the cover."

"But you *have* killed people."

"Yes," he said calmly. "But right now I'm not looking to kill anyone. I need to get into the ME's office, and I need someone to translate Ricky Charles's autopsy findings into lay English for me." He paused, and seemed reluctant to admit, "You're right, I'm one of the good guys, more or less. I'm part of a unit that's so secure we don't even know each other. We only know our handler, who goes by the name Jane Doe, and doesn't appear in any government database that I've ever accessed. Anyway, I haven't been able to get in touch with Jane since late last night, which means I'm low on options here. I'm asking for your help."

"Why can't you reach her?"

"My guess? Because she's dead."

Chapter Four

Chelsea thought she heard something in his voice—pain, maybe, and anger—but she couldn't be sure. He was so brutally controlled that very little broke through.

"I'm sorry," she said, and there was a serious quaver in her voice, because the whole conversation seemed patently unbelievable. Handsome undercover operatives just didn't break into the homes of people like her and ask them for help. They just didn't.

Then again, people like her didn't normally get kidnapped, drugged and rescued either.

"Will you help?" he asked, holding her eyes with his.

"Why me?" she managed to ask, her voice sounding thin and strange. "How did you find me? How did you get in here?"

They weren't the most important questions, but they were the only ones she could manage right then, as a whirl of thoughts jammed her brain and her inner wimp told her to stay the hell away from Fairfax, while her spy-loving self wanted to know more, wanted to know everything.

"The first two questions have the same answer," he said. He reached into his pocket and withdrew a flat plastic square, and flipped it to her.

She caught it on the fly. "My name tag. Which answers how you found me—I'm in the phone book, on Google, however you want to look me up. But it doesn't explain why you came to me."

"Because you work in the ME's office."

"Oh. Right. And that was the only reason?" She knew it was stupid of her to ask, and even stupider to feel a spurt of disappointment.

"The only one I'm admitting to." His lips tipped up in a faint, sad smile, there and gone so quickly she might've thought she'd imagined it if she hadn't seen the unexpected hint of a dimple on one cheek. It didn't exactly make him look boyish and approachable—she had a strong feeling he didn't do boyish or approachable very well—but it definitely stirred her juices, bringing a flare of warmth where such a thing should never have existed.

At best, he was an undercover fed with so few outside ties that he'd willingly gone to jail for an op. At worst, he was lying through his teeth, and really was a murderer, and an escapee.

She knew she should run far and fast. Somehow, though, she couldn't. Instead, she stood and crossed to him, stopping just short of where he stood in the shadows cast by the single lamp that lit the living room. "What, exactly, do you want me to do?"

He glanced at her TV, where the digital display on the cable box showed that it was nearly 7:00 p.m. He muttered a curse. "I don't have time tonight. I've stretched the supply run as long as I can. They'll be expecting me back soon."

At the mention of the others, she looked around in sudden panic, locking on the woods beyond her yard. "Where are they?" Images of al-Jihad and the others crowded her brain. "Are they out there?"

"No." But he didn't elaborate. "Will you help me?"

"Why are you protecting them? Why not tell the cops where they are?"

"Because I'm the one who helped them escape, remember? Why else do you think I had the knockout drops?"

"You—" She broke off as a sinking sensation warned her that she was way out of her depth. Making a sudden decision, she said, "I can't deal with this." She turned for the door. "You have until the count of ten to get the hell out of here. When I hit ten, I'm opening the front door and screaming bloody murder."

This time he didn't try to stop her physically. Instead, he said, "Didn't you wonder why you recovered from the drug so fast and why the doctors couldn't find any trace of it in your blood? Didn't you wonder who called in the nine-one-one and gave the cops your location?"

She stopped, but didn't turn around. "I suppose you can explain that?" She cursed herself for giving him the opening, but he'd nailed the questions she'd been asking herself all day.

"Look at me."

Still cursing herself for a fool, she did exactly that, only to find that he'd moved, so silently she hadn't known he was coming until he was inside her space the way she'd been inside his only moments earlier.

She wanted to back away, but something told her now was not the time to let him know exactly how much his physical presence—and the feelings he kindled inside her—intimidated her. So instead of retreating, she stood her ground and lifted her chin. "Well?"

He leaned in, until their faces were too close together and his breath feathered across her skin.

"I planted a homing device on you, along with a data pellet. Jane—or more likely, one of her people—retrieved the information and the bug, gave you the antidote to the injection, and rearranged the scene a little before calling it in."

Her mouth had gone dry during his recitation, which was too far-out to be true, too consistent with the evidence to be a lie. Heart drumming against her ribs, she said, "If you've got other people on your team, why do you need me?"

His voice was flat when he said, "I only know how to contact Jane. It's safer that way."

Until she gets knocked out of the picture, at which point you're on your own, Chelsea thought, but didn't say. It seemed like a very lonely way to live, and was the sort of detail the movies skimmed over in order to hit the action and danger.

"You've got to have some sort of backup plan, right?"

"Wrong."

Chelsea exhaled a frustrated breath. "There's nobody who can confirm your story?"

"Nobody I trust."

She got the feeling the number of people he trusted could be counted on one finger, and that person was out of commission either temporarily or permanently.

"Why not turn them in?" she asked again. "If you're cut off, then your plan's already shot, right? There's no need to keep going. If you help recapture the escapees, then—"

But he was already shaking his head. "Even in captivity, al-Jihad is threatening this country. He's got people inside Homeland Security. He got to people inside your office. We suspect his network extends much farther than we ever guessed, which is why I had to break him out. He'll make contact with his conspirators now, and he'll be planning something big. I can guarantee that much." His expression went grim and determined. "When those plans are in place, we'll bring down his whole godforsaken network, not just a few players."

"But who is 'we'?" she protested. "You just said you're on your own. If you don't have anyone else you can trust—"

"That's not your concern."

Chilled by his flat pronouncement, Chelsea wrapped her arms around herself. "What about me?"

She didn't know what she wanted him to say, didn't know that anything could possibly make this entire conversation any less unreal than it felt at that moment.

"I saved you," he said flatly. "Now I need your

help. Tomorrow, I want you to ensure that the office will be deserted and the security off-line after hours."

Chelsea couldn't figure out which was worse: that he was asking her to betray Sara and the others by breaking more laws than she could immediately name…or that she was actually considering doing it.

What was wrong with her? She had no proof he was who he said. In fact, logic said he was a criminal and a liar.

"If you were really an undercover agent working for the U.S. government," she said, her voice barely above a whisper, "then I can't imagine you'd come here and tell me that to my face." She looked up at him, baffled, wanting to believe him, but not sure she dared. "You haven't even sworn me to secrecy or anything."

The corners of his mouth twitched, the almost-dimple making it seem as though there was a younger, happier man trapped inside his unemotional shell. "Go ahead and tell your friends about this," he said, daring her. "You don't believe me and you're standing here. What do you think they'll do?"

"Put me on the head-shrink express," she said. "Damn it." He was right. She couldn't tell. Not unless she had proof, and there was only one way to get that proof. She tilted her head, shot him a look from beneath her lashes, and felt her heart begin to pound with fear, with excitement. "Tomorrow night, you said?"

His look was long and slow, until finally he nodded. "Tomorrow. Make sure the place is going to be clear."

"I can do that."

"Yes, but will you?" It was a direct challenge. She met his eyes, and nodded, unspeaking.

"Good." He moved, but instead of moving away from her, as she might have expected once he'd gotten his way, he moved in, closing the gap between them. "You wanted to know why you." It wasn't a question.

Her blood sped in her veins, and prickles of awareness shimmered to life. "Yes." The word was barely a breath, more an invitation than a question as the attraction that she'd felt earlier in the day, when their eyes had connected through a pane of tempered and meshed glass, sprang to life full-blown, even stronger now, and with no glass separating them.

"Yeah," he said, as though she'd answered him far more fully than she'd intended to. "That's why."

Then he leaned in and kissed her, and although she'd seen it coming, knew what he'd intended, she didn't move away, didn't stop him cold. Instead, she uncrossed her arms and flattened her palms on his chest, not to push him away, but to draw him close, her fingers twining in the material of his shirt and holding him fast.

And, even though she knew better, damn it… she kissed him back.

TEMPORARY INSANITY. That was Fax's only excuse for initiating the kiss, and it wasn't much of an excuse to begin with. Then, about three seconds after he'd lost his mind and gone in for a taste of her lips, those very same lips parted and a soft sound escaped her, and she started kissing him back.

After that, there was no excuse. There was only insanity.

She tasted of sweetness, sunshine and laughter, and so many other things he hadn't known in a very long time. Her skin was soft beneath his fingertips when he raised his hands to frame her face, to touch her neck and hair, relearning feelings he'd left behind.

Heat came, and lust. But even the lust was tempered with sweetness. It stole inside him and buoyed his heart, making him feel light and free, while the heat warmed him from within, thawing parts of him that had been cold for so long.

Which wasn't a good thing, he realized with a sudden dash of icy reality. Not where he was going.

"Wait." He broke the kiss, only then realizing that he'd moved in very close to her, that they were plastered together against the living-room wall, his body pressed against hers, hard and needy.

Her face was upturned to his, her lips parted and moist, her eyes bright with arousal and self-awareness, letting him know she knew what he was—or thought she did—and she'd kissed him back anyway.

He forced himself to let her go and move away, remembering to stay out of the window lines, but only barely. His head was spinning, his blood pounding an up-tempo number in his veins, and pretty much everything inside him was clamoring for him to go to her, kiss her again, take whatever she was willing to give.

What was going on with him? He wasn't the kind of guy who lost himself in a kiss, wasn't the type to forget reality in a moment of lust.

Only that was what had just happened, and it'd happened with a woman who was so far out of his present sphere that she might as well have been from another universe entirely. She was the sort of person he was trying to protect—in a general sense—when he did what he did. She was sunlight and family; he was alone in the darkness, and needed to keep it that way.

She was attracted to him, he knew, had been from the first moment they locked eyes. It wouldn't take much for him to get her to take it further, especially after all they'd been through together in the past couple of days. She'd said it herself, she owed him her life. He could lean on that, use it to get what he wanted, what his body was demanding he take, hard and hot and fast.

And that, he thought bitterly, *is the convict talking.*

He'd been playing the scumbag role for so long, through a string of assignments even before the al-Jihad op, that he honestly wasn't sure it was a role anymore. His mother used to warn him and his brothers that if they made faces too often, they'd get stuck that way.

Well, somewhere along the line he'd gotten stuck. He'd not only lost his family, he'd lost most of himself. Worse, he wasn't really sure he minded.

He did, however, mind the idea of using someone like Chelsea for sex when he could offer nothing else but his body.

"Bad idea," he said, voice rough. He jammed his hands in his pockets when they wanted to reach for her, and forced his feet to stay put when they wanted to move. "I don't think—"

A knock at the door had him breaking off with a vicious curse. He'd way overstayed his limit, and was seconds away from being busted.

Eyes locked with his, Chelsea raised her voice and called, "Just a minute." She pushed him toward the kitchen, lowering her voice to whisper, "Go. Meet me here tomorrow, and I'll get you into the ME's office."

She didn't say anything about the kiss, but it buzzed between them like a living, tempting thing.

He hesitated, wanting to tell her to forget about tomorrow night, to say there was another way. But there wasn't. He'd already gone over all his options. Without Jane he had no backup—and the very fact that she'd dropped off the grid was a very bad sign. It suggested that al-Jihad's conspirators had shut her down, maybe even killed her, as he'd said to Chelsea.

What he hadn't said was that if Jane was gone, he was locked in a deadly race. He needed to find the traitors and figure out who he could trust to take them down, before they found and dealt with him. And now he was adding another layer of complication: he had to keep Chelsea safe.

He'd kissed her. There was no way he could consider her collateral damage now. He was a cold bastard, yes, but he wasn't completely bloodless.

Unfortunately, that didn't change the fact that he needed her help.

Making the only decision he could under the circumstances, he nodded and headed for the kitchen door, and the shadows beyond. He trusted his training and instincts to get him out even if the second cop had gone around to the back of the house. With the state forest so close to the back door, it would be easy—too easy if you asked him—for him to slip away, unseen.

He turned in the kitchen doorway. Chelsea's eyes met his, and when they did he felt a punch of heat that was sharper, edgier than it'd been when they kissed. This heat was less about lust and more about territoriality and protectiveness, which were two things he absolutely couldn't afford on this mission.

"See you tomorrow," he said softly. And left.

But no matter how fast he slipped through the shadows and away, no matter how fast he drove the car he'd boosted and filled with stolen provisions, he couldn't escape the knowledge that he'd just made this operation far more complicated than it had been, far more complicated than it ought to be.

He only hoped he could pull it off, because if he couldn't, if al-Jihad succeeded in gathering his forces and launching another terror attack, Fax knew the deaths would be on him.

By the time Chelsea arrived at work after a mostly sleepless night, with her police detail shadowing her until she was safely inside, she had pretty much convinced herself she'd gone a little crazy the night before.

She'd allowed Fax to enter her house and escape again, even though he was a wanted felon. She'd agreed to help him in an investigation that might or might not be legitimate. She'd kissed him and would've offered more than a kiss. But the surveillance team had interrupted to check that she was okay, having thought they'd seen a man's shadow in one of the windows.

She'd definitely lost it.

After dumping her coat and bag in her small cubbyhole of an office and pulling fresh scrubs on over her street clothes for the day ahead, Chelsea went in search of her boss. If anyone would have a levelheaded perspective on the situation, it'd be Sara.

Sara was in her larger, windowed office, frowning over a mountain of paperwork. But when Chelsea knocked on the door frame, she looked up and smiled, her expression tinged with concern. "You're here!"

Chelsea frowned. "Shouldn't I be?"

"Of course, I just—" Sara broke off, shaking her head. "Never mind. You're right. I wouldn't want to be sitting home alone after what you went through. Better for you to be here, working. Keeping your mind off things."

"Exactly," Chelsea said. But the strange thing was, she realized, she didn't totally *want* to keep her mind off what had happened. She wanted to really think about everything that'd happened, dissecting the memories not just for the flush of heat brought by thoughts of Fax, but also so that she could think about what the other men had said and done during her abduction, and what it might mean.

Fax had said al-Jihad had people inside federal law enforcement. What if she could actually do something to help identify the traitors, and prevent al-Jihad from launching the terror attack that Fax seemed convinced was on the horizon?

Or conversely, what if none of that existed and he was just using her for some other purpose? Horror spurted through her veins at the sudden thought that he could be somehow using her to plan the very terror attack he was claiming to want to foil.

But how could she know which was the truth when there was nobody she could ask?

"Chelsea?" Sara leaned forward in her desk chair, looking concerned. "Are you sure you should be here? Your color's off."

To be honest, she was dizzy and on the brink of nausea, but she wasn't going to admit that to her boss, who would send her home, or, worse, to the hospital. That was probably where she should be, only she couldn't bring herself to believe she'd been suckered. She had to believe what Fax had told her, not the least because his explanation fit perfectly with her rescue from the cave. Surely that was evidence that Fax and Jane Doe were real?

Maybe, maybe not. But if what he'd told her was true, then it was her responsibility to help, even though her inner wimp wanted to run and hide.

She took a deep breath and forced her voice steady when she said, "I'm fine, really. What's on the docket for today?"

Sara gave her a long up-and-down look, but eventually nodded, seeming to accept her decision. She ran down the day's pending autopsies, all of which sounded fairly routine.

Chelsea frowned. "What about Jerry and the guards?"

The very thought of cutting into a friend made the nausea spike hard, but she didn't want to be shut out of the investigation because Sara and the others thought she couldn't handle it. She'd find a way to deal.

"They're being taken care of," Sara said tightly, her expression a mix of irritation and sorrow.

"They were turfed somewhere else?" Chelsea

supposed it made sense, given that the Bear Claw ME's office was directly involved in the crime. She could see that the decision had wounded Sara, though her friend's expression made her suspect there was more to it than just the autopsies being sent elsewhere.

Something bad was going on behind the scenes. But what? Chelsea wondered. Did Sara know something more about Rickey's involvement? Was she somehow involved in—

Stop it, Chelsea told herself sternly. *Just stop it now.* There was no way Sara was involved with terrorists. Absolutely not.

"The bodies were kicked up a level to the feds," Sara said with a grimace. "The good news is that Seth got permission to sit in on the autopsies, so we'll have some information flow."

FBI evidence specialist Seth Varitek was married to another of Bear Claw's finest, forensic evidence specialist Cassie Dumont-Varitek. Although Chelsea wasn't as close to the couple as she was to Alyssa and Tucker, she knew and trusted Seth. That meant she could add another name to the list of trusted people who were involved in the investigation.

Which got her wondering whether Fax would take her word on that and let her involve a few other people in his investigation. He'd have to believe that there wouldn't be any leaks, but added cops would spread out the work and the risk, and exponentially increase their chances of success.

It would also mean she wouldn't have to lie to her closest friends.

Chelsea decided she'd talk to Fax about the idea that night. Which, she realized, meant that she'd fully committed inwardly to meeting him and sneaking him into the office, despite her myriad misgivings.

Not wishing to examine that decision—or the reasons behind it—too closely, Chelsea said, "How is the acting mayor handling the situation?"

Sara made a face. "About how you'd expect. Proudfoot is launching a media blitz designed to convince the locals and tourists that it's safe to come to Bear Claw for the big party on Sunday."

Chelsea frowned. "Party? What's— Oh, right. The parade." Each year, Bear Claw hosted its own take on Oktoberfest, designed to kick off the ski season. "I forgot."

"You've had a few other things on your mind," Sara said wryly, then continued, "In addition to his media campaign, Proudfoot is also doing a Riverdance-worthy two-step, simultaneously taking credit for our successes, while making sure everyone knows it was the former mayor's hires who either messed up or were actively engaged in criminal behavior."

"What a prince."

"Yeah, well." Sara's shoulders slumped. "Unfortunately in this case he's not the only one thinking along those lines. I'm expecting another invasion from Infernal Affairs any minute."

Taking that as a hint, Chelsea said, "I'll go look busy, then. Catch you later, and don't let IA get you down."

She had a feeling that it wasn't IA in general, but rather one particular internal investigator who got on Sara's nerves, but she'd learned early on not to ask about Sara's combative relationship with Romo Sampson. That was one of the few topics pretty much guaranteed to put her friend in a bad mood.

It took a while, but eventually Chelsea managed to get back into the swing of her work. She cranked through several routine cases with minimal fuss, labeling and packaging the samples that would be sent out to an off-site lab for testing, and preparing the bodies for release to their families.

She worked efficiently, but compassionately, handling the dead with as much respect as possible under the circumstances, knowing that her work helped bring closure, if not always comfort.

All the while, she was thinking about what had

happened two days earlier and the night before. She was definitely feeling more settled than she had the previous afternoon; it helped immeasurably to know—or to at least think she knew—that Fax wasn't the sort of man the media had portrayed him to be.

She wasn't naive enough to think he wasn't capable of doing what they said he had. He was capable of all that and more. But her instincts said he'd been telling the truth about Jane Doe, his allegiance to the U.S. and his hatred of terrorists.

After so many years of reading about them, she'd finally met an actual spy. Under the circumstances, it seemed silly to find that exciting, yet her excitement built through the course of the day, thinking of him and of the kiss they'd shared.

Then it came to quitting time and reality returned with a crash, warning her that the excitement had been nothing more than her mind's way of not dealing with the fear, of not thinking about what she planned to do that night.

She was putting her career on the line for a guy who'd escaped from the ARX Supermax and taken three convicted terrorists with him. A man who claimed to be one of the good guys, but didn't have a damn thing he could show her to back it up.

Suddenly, the psych ward didn't seem like such a bad idea after all.

Dressed in another snazzy wool coat—this one a deep burgundy that flared at the hem—Sara paused outside Chelsea's cubbyhole office and said, "You want to get something to eat, maybe hang out for a while?"

Nerves skimmed just beneath the surface, flowing alongside guilt at lying to a friend, but even in her preoccupied state, Chelsea could see that Sara looked done-in. She shook her head. "We both know you're hoping I'll say 'no thanks, I'm good.' So I'll say it. No thanks, I'm good."

Sara scrubbed a hand across her face. "It's that obvious? Sorry."

"You've had a rough few days. We all have. It's only natural to want some alone time when you've got half the city breathing down your neck."

"I'm here if you need me, though."

"I know." Chelsea rose and moved around the desk so she could press her cheek to Sara's. "Same goes."

After Sara left, Chelsea fiddled around for a few minutes longer, then started closing up the morgue for the night, powering down the computers and lights, and the nonessential machines. When she set the security system, though, she deliberately took the back door off-line, so her reentry later wouldn't alert the officer on duty at the main desk of the PD, which had a hardwired feed from the security system at the ME's office.

Deliberately rigging the security system gave Chelsea serious queasiness. If—or rather *when*—IA figured out that someone had been inside the morgue after hours, it would be ridiculously easy for the investigators to figure out that she'd been the inside woman. But that didn't stop her. She had to believe she was doing the right thing, even if it might not look that way to the people who knew her best.

If everything went right, she'd be a hero. If not, she'd be unemployed and unemployable. It was her call, her choice.

Stifling the little voice that said she should go straight to Seth and Tucker and tell them about Fax's visit to her house, she collected her police escort and headed home. After the two cops checked out her house and refused her offer of coffee, they left her and went across the street to their cruiser, considering her tucked in safely for the night.

In reality, she was waiting. And jittering.

Amped up, both by the risk she was about to take and by the promise of seeing Fax again, knowing now how he tasted and how his body felt against hers, she moved from one room to the next, unable to settle. Having seen him do it the night before, she avoided the windows, not wanting the cops to see her pacing one minute, gone the next. She tried to copy his movements, too—the way his footsteps had been almost silent, and how he had seemed perfectly balanced, ready to fight or flee at a moment's notice.

Or rather, ready to fight, not flee. He wasn't the sort to back down from any challenge.

Stop it, she told herself. *He's not a character from some book or movie that you're free to have a crush on. He's a real guy, and he's not yours.* Which was true, she knew. Fax might have asked for her help because he had nowhere else to turn, and he might want her physically, but he'd never stick around or ask her to come away with him. She knew that like she knew her own name, her own weaknesses.

That didn't mean she couldn't indulge for the duration, though, she thought, imagining him naked, remembering the taste and feel of him, the—

"Chelsea."

She gasped and spun, and there he was, standing in her darkened kitchen doorway with the night at his back. He was wearing dark jeans that fit like they'd been made for him, along with heavy hiking boots and a sweater the same blue as his eyes. He wore the lined leather jacket he'd had on the night before, along with black gloves because the night was crisp, the air hinting at more rain, or maybe wet snow.

She imagined he had his gun tucked at the small of his back, and found that dangerous detail to be staggeringly sexual.

His eyes locked on her and went hot for a second, flaring with the same heat that slammed through her, warning that the rest of it was all rationalization, that her first and best reason for doing what she was about to do was because he'd asked. Because she wanted him.

The kiss they'd shared the night before resonated in the air between them, almost a tangible thing. Electricity sparked, sizzling a wordless question of what they were going to do about it, where they would go from there.

Then his eyes blanked back to icy cool, and he said only, "You ready to go?"

She took a deep breath and nodded, and when he turned and glided out into the night, she followed him into the forest behind her house and didn't look back.

Chapter Five

Fax cursed himself inwardly as he led Chelsea along a short loop through the woods to where he'd stashed the nonstolen, properly registered car that al-Jihad had procured through his network of area contacts, none of whom Fax had met yet.

This is a really bad idea, he thought. He should've stayed back at the hideout, working on getting Muhammad to trust him. Instead, he was following a lead he didn't have nearly enough manpower to do justice to, one that would most likely threaten Chelsea's job, if not her life.

He'd tried to talk himself out of the plan a few times over the course of the day. Okay, more like once every ten minutes or so, which was about how often he'd thought about her.

He'd thought of how it had felt to kiss her the night before, and he'd thought of doing it again, of working his way down her body, tasting every inch of creamy skin. Of losing himself inside her.

He'd thought of her as he'd helped Lee and Muhammad set up the small cabin they were using, located high on a ridge that overlooked Bear Claw Canyon and led up to the mountain used by the city's main ski resort. They'd outfitted the cottage with the supplies he'd stolen, along with boxes of other essentials that'd appeared out of nowhere, reconfirming that al-Jihad's reach remained long, his subjects loyal.

And he'd thought of her as he'd looked in the terrorist leader's eyes and seen the cold sanity there, the murderous rage, the desire to kill the whole country, and the American way of life.

This was far too dangerous a situation for Chelsea. It was too much to ask of anyone, never mind someone like her. She was sweetness and innocence, America and apple pie. She was all the things people like al-Jihad wanted to wipe from the face of the earth.

It wasn't right. Unfortunately, he still hadn't been able to reach Jane—the lines of communication had gone dead, and the very nature of his cover meant that he didn't have access to the information he'd once had at his fingertips. He was going to have to do things the old-fashioned way, through hands-on investigation.

Even worse, based on a few things Muhammad had let slip, he suspected that they didn't have much time left. Whatever al-Jihad was planning, it was going to happen Sunday morning, which was less than seventy-two hours away.

If Fax thought there was a chance that turning himself in and leading the authorities to the escapees' hideout would prevent an attack, he would've done just that. But logic and experience said that the plan was already in place, and the underlings had their orders. Even if al-Jihad and the others were back in custody, the attack would be carried out on schedule.

Fax needed to know who else was involved. He needed to take them down all at once. That was the only way he was going to save lives. And for that, he needed more information on Rickey Charles. Which meant he needed Chelsea.

When they reached the dark bulk of the car, he used the keyless remote to pop the locks and got her door open for her.

He caught the flash of surprise in her eyes. "Thanks."

"My mother taught me well."

Once he was in the driver's seat and they were headed down the road into town, she said, "Does she know…you know. What you're doing?"

"She knows I'm in jail for murder," he said shortly, wishing he'd never mentioned her. This wasn't the time or place for getting-to-know-you chitchat.

The slip was just another sign of how Chelsea's involvement was messing him up, blurring the line between the man he'd been and the one he had to be now.

He glanced over and caught her looking at his profile.

When their eyes met, she looked away. "In other words, you don't want to talk about your family."

"What's the point?" When that came out sounding far harsher than he'd intended, he muttered a curse, took a breath, and forced himself to back it down a notch. "I'm sorry, I don't mean to be a jerk. It's just I don't want—" He broke off, not sure anymore what he did and didn't want. "Damn it."

"I'm the one who should be sorry." She looked away, so her voice was slightly muffled when she said, "This isn't a date. There's no reason for us to get to know each other better. I'm just…" She shrugged. "I was just trying to make it seem a little more normal, I guess. Which is silly, really, because this is anything but normal."

"You can say that again," he said, and let the conversation lag as he sent the car through the twisty streets of Bear Claw, headed back to the loading dock where they'd met.

Strange thing was, part of him wanted to do the

small-talk thing, wanted to get to know her better. The urge was separate from the attraction, too, like he was looking to take a piece of her sweetness for himself by pretending he was the sort of man she'd be with if she'd had a choice in the matter.

Because really, he was under no illusions on that front. Once upon a time he'd been the sort of guy nice girls went for, but those days were long gone.

"We're here," he said as he pulled up to the back dock of the ME's office, then winced and said, "Sorry. You knew that."

She looked over at him. Her chocolate-brown eyes were very serious, but her full lips twitched at the corners, turning up in a half smile that held more resignation than humor. "Let's agree to stop apologizing, okay? This is weird for both of us."

He nodded. "Thank you. For doing this, I mean. And I promise I'll do my best to keep you safe."

"I know." She stared at the doors leading to the morgue, and he could tell she was thinking about what'd happened there two days earlier, about her friend who'd been killed. About what might've happened to her, what would've happened if she hadn't lucked into the middle of an undercover op.

"You want to bail out on this?" he asked.

"Of course I do." But she popped open the door and unhooked her seat belt. "I'd be stupid if I didn't. But you need help."

She got out of the car before he could follow his impulse to call her back, to call it off and come up with another plan.

Only there was no other plan. And they had less than three days to root out al-Jihad's conspirators and prevent what he feared would be a major terror attack.

CHELSEA HAD WORKED odd hours in the morgue before, during crisis situations and high-priority cases, when the cops needed answers pronto. She'd stayed late a night or two doing paperwork as well. But she'd never come back in after hours and been the only one there.

Even the cleaning crews were gone for the night—which, of course, was why they'd waited until so late to come. But the silence was creepy, the dim lights even worse.

For the first time, her job seemed less about compassion and more about corpses. Her imagination started playing tricks on her, showing flickers of motion at the edges of her peripheral vision, and sending the sly scrape of a footstep to her ears, just below the threshold of hearing.

Then a hand grabbed on to her arm, and she jumped a mile, giving a little squeak of fear.

"Shh," Fax ordered. "It's me." He shook her arm. "Hold it together, okay?"

She concentrated on the feel of his touch, the strength of his fingers, firm yet gentle on her flesh, and warm even through her shirt and light jacket. Using those sensations to steady herself, to anchor herself, she nodded. "I'm okay. What do you want to see first?"

"Did Rickey Charles have a computer station of his own? An office, or a cube or something?"

"This way." She led him down a short corridor, gesturing to doors as they passed. "This is Sara's office. Mine." She stopped outside the next door down. "Rickey's."

Fax paused. "Have the crime scene techs been here already?"

She frowned. "You know, I'm not sure. Sara said something about them being delayed."

"Big surprise," he muttered. "Al-Jihad has friends everywhere, it seems." He glanced at her. "You got any nonpowdered latex gloves?"

"Of course." She went and grabbed a handful from the morgue, feeling strange and ill at ease in her own space.

Fax was waiting for her in the hallway when

she returned. She practically shoved the gloves at him. "Here. Let's hurry."

He didn't say anything, just looked at her, and his icy reserve softened just the barest hint around the edges. "I know we said no more apologies, but I really am sorry I dragged you into this."

"Didn't stop you from doing it, though, did it?" She pushed at his shoulder, aiming him at the door. "Just do whatever you need to do."

"I'll be quick."

And he *was* quick, she realized over the next forty minutes as she watched him go through Rickey's work life inside and out, and then turn his attention to Sara and Jerry. He even went through the desk of their forty-something clerical assistant, Della Jones. She was a divorced mother of two who sometimes dated their thirty-something meat wagon driver, Bradley.

She was definitely *not* a terrorist.

Then again, what do I know about terrorists? Chelsea thought as she hovered over Fax's shoulder, her stomach in knots, half afraid he wouldn't find anything, half afraid that he would.

When he bypassed her office and headed for the morgue itself, she said, "You don't want to toss my office?"

He stopped and turned, his strong body silhouetted in the dim emergency lights that were the only thing illuminating the hallways so late at night. "Why?" His voice seemed almost disembodied. "Should I be worried about you?"

"You seem to be worried about everybody else." Her voice was sharper than she'd intended, the irritation closer to the surface than she'd realized. "I told you Jerry was harmless. And Sara's my friend. She wouldn't ever in a million years do something like this. Never mind Della, who wouldn't hurt a flea."

He approached her, his footsteps nearly silent on the marble tiles lining the hallway. Stopping very near her, he leaned down and whispered, "It's my job to be worried about everyone and everything. If I stop worrying, then I stop breathing."

For a second his lips hovered above hers and she thought he was going to kiss her. She felt the zip of heat in a time and place it shouldn't have existed.

Then he moved away, turned on his heel, and headed for the autopsy theater. "Show me the computers in here, and how to hack in. I need to see the guards' autopsies."

"You were there when they died. What will the autopsies tell you that you don't already know?" Her voice was starting to crack around the edges from the strain of the past few days. She was getting ragged, beginning to think she'd made a mistake.

He was investigating her coworkers, her friends. And she was helping him.

He might be looking for a traitor, but she already was one.

"Chelsea." He was near her again without her having been aware that he'd moved. He touched a finger beneath her chin and used it to tip her face up to his, not for a kiss, but so that she was looking into his eyes when he said, "This is necessary. I swear it."

The thing was, she believed him. Was that her instincts talking or something else?

She stepped away and nodded. "Come on. I'll get you into the files."

Five minutes later, he made a low sound of satisfaction. "Gotcha."

"What?" She crowded behind him, and leaned over his shoulder. "What do you see?"

"Here." He pointed to a line of autopsy notes. "This isn't right. I know for a fact that this guy had a bullet in him, yet the autopsy only mentions the broken neck." He glanced at her, his face too close to hers, his eyes going a little sad for her. "The autopsy was rigged. You know what that means, right?"

"That we're not your problem," she said.

He narrowed his eyes. "Excuse me?"

She gestured around the morgue. "The state made us ship out the autopsies. They said we were too close to the case, that we had to pass the bodies up the chain."

He went very still. "Who did the autopsies?"

"The FBI."

"Hell."

"Which means—" She broke off, realizing exactly what it meant, and echoed his, "Hell."

"Okay, we're done here," he said suddenly, powering down the machine. "Let's go."

She didn't even bother to ask about the rush, just followed him numbly out to the car. It wasn't until they were back on the road headed to her place that he finally said, "What's wrong?"

All of it, she wanted to say. *It's all wrong.*

"The autopsy was overseen by a friend of mine," she said softly, thinking of Cassie's husband, Seth. "Someone I trust."

"Trusted, you mean. Past tense."

She shook her head. "I don't know. None of this makes any sense." She glanced over at Fax. "I was going to ask you—beg you, really—to turn yourself in to him. I thought we could trust him, that he'd be a good guy to have on our side."

"And now?"

"Now I don't know what to think."

He reached across the distance separating them, and closed his fingers over hers. "Welcome to my world. Do yourself a favor and get out as soon as you can."

"Just tell me when and where, and I'll take a flying leap off this bus," she said, and almost meant it. But she'd seen too much death and comforted too many grieving families to walk away now, when she might be able to do something to prevent a terrorist attack and the deaths it would bring.

She sighed, realizing that her conscience could apparently override her inner wimp and almost wishing it couldn't. "What next?" she asked.

He looked at her for a moment, his eyes intent, and something moved in their depths, making her wonder what he saw when he looked at her. A nice girl? A small life? Or something more?

But he said only, "Let's get you home before we push our luck too far."

He walked her through the woods to her back door, proving once again that her police protection was more for show than anything else.

Once she had the kitchen door open, she paused. "Do you want to come in?"

It was a foolish offer, a sign of just how confused she was inside, how much she'd blurred the lines between date and danger, adventure and stupidity. Fiction and reality.

He shook his head, his eyes holding hers. "I shouldn't."

Not *I can't,* but *I shouldn't.*

"You're probably right," she agreed, but she didn't move out of the doorway.

He stepped up onto the landing. With her standing a tread higher on the threshold, the move put them eye-to-eye.

Electricity buzzed in the air. Chemistry. Maybe it was a pointless, futureless, mad attraction, but in that moment the logic didn't seem to matter.

Only the heat mattered.

"I've gotta go," he said, but didn't.

"I know," she said, and even though it made absolutely no sense, what she really meant was, *Come inside.*

He leaned in and touched his lips to hers, a fleeting touch, there and gone so quickly that she might've imagined it, except there was no imagining the arcing shock of sensation, and the ripe, full flavor of him.

She moved to deepen the kiss.

He stepped away, shook his head. "I'm sorry."

Backing away from her, he turned and crossed her backyard, then slipped into the forest. And was gone.

AS HE RETRIEVED his vehicle and set off for the deep-woods hideout where al-Jihad and the others were hiding, Fax tried to tell himself that it'd been the right choice to reveal himself to Chelsea and recruit her help. She was a necessary asset at a time when he was cut off from his normal channels.

Despite that logic and the fact that he'd done everything he could think of to ensure her safety within the dangerous circumstances surrounding her, he couldn't outrun the growing certainty that he was playing it wrong, taking advantage of someone who deserved better, who shouldn't be part of his world.

Then again, that was part of the horror of terrorism: it brought evil into everyday life.

Unfortunately, that sometimes meant that the good guys had to bring the war into the picket-fenced backyards of America and apple pie. Fax understood the need. He'd dealt with the emotions—what few he had left—long ago, consoling himself with the knowledge that for every innocent life lost during one of his ops, several hundred other people would live on oblivious, never knowing how close they'd come to death.

Usually he neither liked nor disliked the necessity; he simply accepted it. Now, though, he was caught up in it, worried about it, thinking more about the danger to Chelsea than the menace of al-

Jihad and the terrorist leader's plan, which he could sense taking shape around him but couldn't define.

He knew he had three days—*make that two and a half now,* he thought, glancing at the in-dash display, which showed that it was well past 2:00 a.m. But although he knew approximately when, he had no idea of where or how, no idea what sort of attack was being planned. Without those details, the time line was next to useless.

Complicating things even further was Jane's continued silence. He felt a pang of grief for the woman who'd given him purpose—and absolution—after Abby's death.

He knew Jane wouldn't thank him for the grief, though, so he focused on what she would've considered far more important—the information disruption caused by her disappearance and how to circumvent that limitation.

Stop stalling and come up with a plan, Fairfax, she would've said.

With her out of the loop, he didn't have the luxury of knowing a response could be up and running with the snap of a finger. Worse, he strongly suspected she'd been betrayed from within the core of the few people she trusted. She was too smart to be taken out by anything short of betrayal.

If al-Jihad's compatriots were strong enough to

do that, Fax knew they were easily strong enough to make him quietly disappear if he showed up on their radar screens. Especially given that they had someone inside the FBI, as evidenced by the fudged autopsy records. All of which meant he couldn't risk contacting anyone in the federal food chain, for fear of revealing himself to one of the conspirators.

"In other words, I'm on my own," he said as he bounced his way up the narrow lane to where they'd been hiding the cars, and from there hiking up to the cabin. "As usual."

Only it wasn't business as usual, not really, because he had Chelsea on his conscience and in his head.

"You'd better focus," he warned himself as he climbed out of the car and popped the trunk to retrieve the bulging knapsack that had ostensibly been his reason for the midnight errand.

He had to get the woman out of his head, had to get himself into the game.

But as he hiked the half mile farther into the forest to the cabin, he couldn't stop thinking of Chelsea, of the way her short, chestnut-streaked hair brushed the edges of her jaw, and how her brown eyes sparked when she smiled at him, when she argued with him.

Most of all, he couldn't stop remembering the

taste of her skin and mouth, the feel of her curving, feminine body pressed against him.

By the time he reached the encampment, where the plain, square cabin was covered in camo netting and pine branches, and ringed with deadly security sensors, he was more than tempted to turn the hell around and go back for her. But that was attraction talking, not logic, so he kept going, pushing through the cabin door, his senses on alert for any telltale changes, any hint that the situation he was walking into wasn't the one he'd left hours earlier.

Al-Jihad and Muhammad sat at the long table in the center of the main room, which was heaped with encrypted schematics and computer print-outs, and home to four laptops run by a lean, dark-haired stranger.

Fax stopped just inside the doorway and scowled. "Who the hell is that? And where's the lemming?"

Al-Jihad glanced from Fax to the stranger and back, his expression inscrutable. "Lee is off on an errand. And this is one of my consultants." Which didn't explain a damn thing.

Fax wanted to ask more, but he also wanted to get close enough to look at those schematics, to see if he could ID the target. Problem was, he didn't know how far he could push without risking his cover. Al-Jihad and Muhammad seemed to accept his professed hatred of the establishment, and seemed to buy that he wasn't just an anarchist, he was so in love with violence that he was willing to target innocent civilians, as long as it made the government look bad. The terrorist leader and his second in command had given Fax small assignments and seemed willing to let him into their discussions, but only to a point.

He had to wonder, though, whether they were playing him just as thoroughly as he'd been playing them. What was he to them? he wondered. An asset, a tool to be used as a later distraction…or something else? Something more sinister?

Unfortunately, in the absence of other information, his best bet was to keep playing along, watching his back and gathering what information he could.

Senses humming, mind clicking over the options, he took a couple of steps toward the table. "Anything I can help with?"

Al-Jihad looked up at him, and something sparked in the depths of his dead black eyes. "Another time, perhaps."

Fax shrugged. "No biggie. I'll go unpack."

He kept his senses revved as he unloaded six-packs of beer and soda from his knapsack to the fridge. He caught a few words of the conversation, enough to realize they weren't speaking English.

When he stuck his head back through the kitchen door, the conversation cut off abruptly and the men turned to look at him.

"What do you want?" the stranger asked, not bothering to hide his irritation.

"Just checking if either of you wanted something to eat," Fax said with a hint of wary deference in his voice, playing the part of a scared lackey who knew damn well his life was subject to the whims of the terrorist leader.

"No," al-Jihad spat. "Go check the perimeter."

"Will do." Fax made a production of pulling his jacket back on as protection against the sharp wind outside and headed for the door.

On the way past, though, he managed to get a look at the papers on the table. He didn't recognize the schematics, but beneath them was a flyer of some sort, and he caught a single word.

Parade.

Chapter Six

Chelsea slept poorly and woke with a creepy feeling lodged between her shoulder blades. Then again, was there any wonder she felt unsettled? She'd broken into her own office and let a fugitive search Sara's office and scour their computer system.

Doing the wrong thing for the right reason is still doing the wrong thing, her conscience nagged as she showered and dried off, and then did her best to cover up the dark, worried circles beneath her eyes.

Her conscience was right. Unfortunately, she had no clue what the right thing to do would be. This was all so far out of her normal mode of operation, she didn't even know where to start.

The nerves stayed high as she got dressed, choosing sturdy jeans and lace-up boots because they made her feel a little armored-up, and a rust-brown turtleneck sweater that made her eyes look more caramel than brown. Feeling pretty was another layer of armor.

The thought of needing her defenses on high alert put a twist in her stomach. Then the doorbell rang, and the twist became a knot.

"Oh!" She took a couple of steps toward the door, then stopped at the sight of a big, shadowy figure through the curtained window.

She couldn't see many details through the gauze, but immediately knew that it wasn't Fax. For one, the man was ringing at the front door rather than picking the lock on the back. For another, he was bigger than Fax, both taller and broader.

Starting to panic now, she backed up a step, trying to decide between calling for help and trying to escape on her own.

He rang the doorbell again, and knocked. Then called, "Chelsea? It's Seth Varitek."

Seth! Her breath whistled out on a gust of relief and she was halfway across the room when she stalled. Wait a minute. Seth was FBI. Someone in the FBI had falsified the report of an autopsy he'd overseen. What if he were involved?

No, she told herself. Impossible. He was Cassie's husband, part of the gang. He was a decorated expert and had worked some of the highest-profile cases in the country. There was no way he could possibly be involved with al-Jihad.

Still, she stayed in place, frozen with indecision, afraid to trust her own gut anymore.

"Chelsea?" Seth's voice had gone worried, edged with professional calm. "You've got a ten-count to answer before I come through this door."

Finally she moved, not because of the threat, but because he was Seth. A friend. She trusted him. She wasn't cold like Fax. She couldn't just turn her heart on and off.

"Hey!" She opened the door a crack and invited him inside, staying behind the panel, keeping her body shielded in case someone shot at her from the street, like her surveillance team had taught her to do.

The big man's expression cleared some when he saw her, but his eyes stayed pensive and he didn't move to come inside. "What took you so long?"

Seth was a big, dark bear of a man with brush-cut black hair and strong, almost forbidding features. He was wearing jeans and a blue sweat-shirt beneath a Rockies logo jacket, suggesting he was off duty, but his holstered weapon and the badge clipped to his belt said otherwise.

"What—" Chelsea's voice faltered, but she forced the words. "What's going on?"

He gave her a long, measured look, as if to say *you tell me,* but answered simply, "Tucker asked me to pick you up. Romo Sampson wants to talk to you."

"Oh." She closed her eyes on an internal groan.

The hotshot IAD investigator was rumored to have no conscience when it came to hounding—and taking down—other cops. He also, Chelsea suspected, had a grudge against the ME's department, going back to right about the time Sara had dated and dumped him.

This wasn't going to be good.

"I could've driven myself," she said faintly, focusing on the immediate problem rather than looking ahead. "I'm not much of a flight risk."

She meant the latter as a weak joke, but even as she said it she realized it wasn't exactly true. The night before, she hadn't just strayed over the line between legal and illegal, she'd blown it up and set fire to the remains. There was no reason they shouldn't consider her a risk.

Heck, if Fax appeared in her kitchen doorway right then and crooked a finger, she'd be sorely tempted to take off and not look back. She'd follow him into the woods…and that was where the fantasy dissolved.

She couldn't go with him to the fugitives' camp, and he had to maintain his presence there.

"It's no big deal," Seth said easily.

It took her a couple of seconds to figure out that he was talking about giving her a ride, not her relationship with a man he didn't even know she was in continued contact with. Not that there was a relationship. There was merely a wish that the situation could have been different. Then again, under other circumstances, she and Fax never would've crossed paths.

Chelsea told herself that probably would've been for the best, which made her sad.

"You ready to go?" the big FBI agent asked. Only it wasn't really a question.

"Of course." She grabbed her coat and followed him out.

Her stomach churned with nerves as she locked the door and walked with Seth to his truck. He hadn't said it, but she knew there was another reason Tucker had asked Cassie's husband to pick her up and drive her to IAD: he'd wanted her to have someone outside Bear Claw law enforcement to talk to, if she felt like she needed it.

Problem was, Seth might be outside the Bear Claw PD, but he wasn't beyond al-Jihad's reach.

As she climbed into the truck and waited for Seth to start the engine, Chelsea wrestled with herself.

She and Fax needed help, whether or not he wanted to admit it. And though it was probably the wimp talking, Chelsea readily admitted to herself that she would feel better if they could bring Seth and a handpicked few of her friends on board. It would give their investigation a sense of legitimacy, and it'd mean she wouldn't have to lie to her friends, which she hated doing.

Problem was, after last night she knew Fax would never, ever agree to bring in other people, especially not someone from the Bear Claw PD or FBI. And she didn't know him well, but she could guess that if she told them the truth and Fax found out, she'd never see him again. More importantly, she wasn't a hundred percent certain it'd be safe to involve the others.

She trusted her friends, but the evidence said she couldn't trust everyone around them. So as Seth backed out of her driveway and the surveillance vehicle fell in behind them, she tried to figure how to get the information she needed without asking questions that would reveal too much.

"Can I ask you something?" she said finally, knowing she'd have to keep it vague.

The look Seth sent in her direction warned that he wasn't fooled for a second. "Sure. Anything."

"Say someone was working undercover—and I mean deep undercover," she began, hoping she wasn't making a huge mistake. "What sort of fail-safes would there be if he lost contact with his handler?"

"What agency?"

"Any one," she said, dodging.

They drove in silence for nearly a mile before Seth muttered a curse under his breath. "What's his contact's name?"

It wasn't a promise of help or secrecy, but within their circle of friendship, that was exactly what it amounted to.

"Jane Doe," Chelsea said softly, hoping she hadn't just made the biggest mistake of her life.

THE HIDDEN CABIN hummed with activity as the plans for the terrorist attack started coming together.

At least Fax got the sense that the scheme was getting nailed down. He didn't know for certain because al-Jihad and Muhammad were keeping him as far out of the loop as possible, using him for information gathering and supply runs, and telling him almost nothing.

Not that Fax could blame them from a strategic point of view—it only made sense to give the new guy the crap jobs. But that meant he was stuck in limbo, part of the plan, yet not. It wasn't enough, damn it. He needed the names of the people on the inside who were involved.

Then and only then would he know who he could trust and who he couldn't.

Additional manpower and supplies arrived

midmorning seemingly out of nowhere, which only added to Fax's frustration.

He couldn't figure out how al-Jihad was contacting his confederates, which meant he was missing a major piece of the puzzle. And if the terrorists were keeping their communication method secret from him, there was a good bet they were keeping other things hidden.

Unfortunately, he didn't dare snoop. Muhammad and al-Jihad were on high alert, as were the five other silent men who moved into and out of the cabin, casting furtive looks in Fax's direction, but not answering any of his greetings. The last member of their group—twitchy, weasely Lee Mawadi—had been growing increasingly twitchy by the hour. Worse, he'd taken to watching Fax, following him around as though the higher-ups had assigned him as a babysitter.

Fax didn't like the thought any more than he liked the man.

Were they keeping tabs on him just to be safe or did they suspect something? *Scratch that,* Fax thought to himself as he bent over his latest task of sawing foot-long pieces of pipe that he could only assume would be turned into bombs over the next two days. *Guys like these are always suspicious— that's what keeps them alive and free. Question is, what's made them extra suspicious now?*

He didn't think the authorities were anywhere close to their hiding spot—that would've brought a different kind of tension. No, this felt more like they were holding out for an answer or a piece of information that would make or break the next step in their game.

But what information? Where was it coming from? And how the hell were they getting it?

Fax wanted to shake the answers out of somebody, but he didn't dare. He could only focus on his task, too aware of the lemming sitting across from him, winding wire for a detonator coil while he divided his attention between the chatter of a daytime talk show on the small TV in the corner, and the drone of voices coming from the back of the four-room cabin.

Fax knew where each of the men were and how they were armed. He had a plan in mind if things went suddenly south—he knew what weapons he'd try for and where his escape routes were. But those were academic exercises for the most part, because experience had taught him that when things went bad, they usually spun right past contingencies and into the realm of action-reaction real fast.

So he stayed ready for action, knowing it might be the difference between life and death—not just his own life, but those of hundreds, probably thousands of innocents who'd be planning to be part of whatever parade the terrorists targeted.

He couldn't warn the authorities yet, he knew. Not until and unless there was no possible option for apprehending al-Jihad and the others mid-crime. He did, however, fully intend to make sure Chelsea was nowhere near the planned attack.

He couldn't save everyone. But he'd damn well save her.

"Fairfax."

It wasn't until he heard Muhammad call his name from the doorway of the back room that Fax realized the air in the little cabin had changed, going from one of waiting to one of decision.

Fine tension shivered across his skin, but he played it cool, setting aside the length of pipe he'd been working on. "Yeah?"

"In here." Muhammad disappeared back into the room.

Fax found himself trading a look with Lee. If it'd been anyone other than the lemming, he might've asked whether the other man knew what was going on. But it wasn't, so he didn't. He just headed into the back room.

He was two steps in when a heavy blow came out of nowhere and struck him across the back of the head.

Fax shouted and spun, grabbing for the

weapon. Al-Jihad himself wielded the short club, his dead eyes alight with killing rage as he hissed, "Traitor!" and came at Fax again.

The second blow caught him in the temple and sent him to his hands and knees, where he braced himself, retching and reeling, not able to run or fight or do anything but howl with the knowledge that his cover was somehow blown, that…

A third blow caught him below the ear and he collapsed into darkness.

He surfaced what seemed like a long time later, pulled to semiconsciousness by the sound of someone saying Chelsea's name.

He stirred and groaned when he heard her name again, and crazily wondered if she was there. But he quickly realized that it wasn't Chelsea herself. It was someone asking him about her. And that was a big problem.

Cracking open his eyes, he squinted into the too-bright light at his interrogator, and recognized Muhammad.

Rage flared when he realized the terrorists knew that he and Chelsea were connected. He was suffused with an overwhelming urge to rip into Muhammad for daring to even say her name. Moments later, though, he blearily realized that he wasn't ripping into anything any time soon. He was securely bound to a chair set in the middle of the cabin's back room. His head lolled, his consciousness was furred with drugs, and he could barely hear the questions Muhammad was firing at him.

His slurred answer was anatomically impossible.

Infuriated, Muhammad backhanded him, then spat in his face. He turned to someone out of Fax's line of sight, and said, "We learned our lesson from the traitor bitch before she died. We need leverage. Pick up the medical examiner and bring her here."

Fax roared at the confirmation of Jane's death, and the implied threat that they were going to torture Chelsea in order to force him to talk. Pushing with his legs, he lunged at the bastard, and succeeded only in toppling his chair sideways. His head slammed into the floorboards, and the world went dim for a while—a few minutes, maybe longer.

When the universe sharpened around him, he was alone.

Chelsea! Fax's heart jammed his throat and adrenaline spiked, chasing the last of the drugs from his bloodstream. He started struggling against his bonds, shouting curses and threats. But there was no answer. The men were long gone.

But how long? He didn't know, couldn't guess,

could only yank against the zip ties that held him
fast, knowing that he needed to get free, needed
to get to Chelsea before al-Jihad and his men did.

If he didn't, she'd be dead.

THE GOOD NEWS, Chelsea realized soon after she
sat down in a PD conference room opposite Romo
Sampson, was that Internal Affairs apparently had
no clue she'd been in the ME's office after hours
the night before.

The bad news was that she'd all but confessed
it to Seth on the ride over. Guilt stung at the suspicion that she should've kept her mouth shut, as
she'd promised Fax she would. She trusted Seth
not to say or do anything that'd get her in trouble
unless he thought it was absolutely necessary, but
she suspected there might be a pretty big difference between Seth's idea of "absolutely necessary" and her own.

She had to face it, she was no good at this spy
stuff. She'd caved under the first real pressure
she'd experienced. But then again, why should
she have expected anything different? This wasn't
a game, wasn't an adventure or a story. This was
real life and death, a threat to her career, her own
safety and that of the people she loved.

Of course she'd caved. She was a wimp.

"Do you need to take a break and get some coffee

or something?" the IAD investigator said dryly, warning Chelsea that she'd zoned out on him mid-question. For all she knew, she'd been snoring.

"Sorry." She smothered a yawn. "I haven't been sleeping well." For a variety of reasons, none of which she intended to share with IAD.

Aside from her somewhat dented loyalty to Fax—and her belief that Seth was going to do right by what she'd told him—there was no way she was putting Sara and the ME's office any further under the political crosshairs than it already was. She might be playing fast and loose with the career that had once been her life, but she wasn't going to do the same with her friends' jobs.

"So," Sampson prompted, "you were describing the van ride after your abduction."

He was a long, lean stretch of a man, with wide-palmed hands that fit with the rumor that he'd gone to college on a basketball scholarship and was headed in the direction of the NBA when a knee injury had ended the dream. His mid-brown hair was finger-tousled and in need of a trim, and his pleasant, regular features would've passed for attractive if it hadn't been for his eyes, which were a very pale hazel and seemed to stare straight through whoever he was looking at.

The effect was off-putting in the extreme. Add

to that the few details Chelsea knew about the end of his and Sara's short-lived affair, plus the power he wielded through IAD, and he was downright intimidating.

At least he would've been, she realized, if she hadn't spent the past few days learning out of necessity how to stand up to Fax, who was just as intimidating and wasn't bound by the PD's code of conduct. Where Romo Sampson was civilized in his pressure, Fax was anything but.

"I've told you everything I remember," Chelsea said to Sampson now. "Twice. I'm not sure how going through it a third time is going to help."

Sampson stared at her for a long, considering moment. Then he glanced down at his notes and muttered something under his breath.

Fax did the same thing when he was annoyed with her, she realized, and couldn't help the warm little bubble that rose in her chest at the thought she was learning to recognize his mannerisms. She was trying not to count the hours until dark, until she figured there was a very good chance he'd sneak through her back door to see her.

And *hello,* she acknowledged inwardly, she had it bad. She was in full-blown crush mode for Jonah Fairfax—undercover, here-today-gone-tomorrow agent who needed her for her connections and maybe wanted her for her body, and that was it.

She'd accidentally become a Bond girl, and everybody knew they never got their man.

"Are we done here?" she blurted, interrupting Sampson mid-question.

Surprise flashed in his pale hazel eyes, followed by irritation. "We're not even close to done, and your boss assured me that you'd be cooperative."

"We both know Sara said nothing of the sort," she said, fixing him with a look that warned him she knew at least some of what had happened between him and her friend.

He scowled. "I was referring to Mayor Proudfoot."

Ouch. Chelsea winced at the direct hit, but the score didn't stop her from pushing back her chair and rising. "Look, can you honestly say I haven't cooperated? I've answered all your questions, haven't I?"

"To a point," he conceded. "But you're not telling everything, are you? Which leads me to ask myself who you're trying to protect. Is it Sara or someone else?" He leaned forward. "How well did you actually know Rickey Charles?"

She met his cool-eyed stare. "You're on the wrong track, Sampson."

"So put me on the right track."

"I'm sorry, I can't help you." She gathered her

coat and bag. "You know where to find me, but don't bother unless you have something new to ask me."

Knowing she was skirting, if not actually crossing, the line career-wise, she left without waiting for his answer. Fuming, but trying not to be afraid, she headed back to the ME's office where she hoped she could find some sanity in the familiar routine of doing her job.

The bodies of the dead didn't give up their secrets easily, but at the same time, they didn't play games, not really. In contrast, she couldn't help feeling as though she'd inadvertently gotten caught up in far more contests than she'd intended to, or even been aware of. For a small person who'd always had a relatively minor impact on her corner of the world, she was suddenly playing bit parts in more dramas than she'd realized at first.

Al-Jihad and his men had used her and discarded her, thinking her dead. Fax had rescued her so he could use her to gain access to information, and as an ally, albeit one of fairly limited means. She suspected Tucker's appearance at her hospital bedside and Seth's offer of a ride that morning were more than friendly support, which suggested they knew there was something going on with her. Enter Romo Sampson, who was sure of it, but wasn't sure who was involved or how, and was convinced that Chelsea knew both. Add to that Sara, who was fighting for her department and had been subtly pressuring Chelsea to play along and not make political waves, little realizing that such a hope had long since been dashed.

On the outskirts of all that were other dramas, other bit players, like Jerry and his ski-bunny girlfriend; Rickey Charles, who'd been a snake, but hadn't deserved to die; and the four guards who'd been killed during the jailbreak.

So many people's lives were already intertwined, so many lives already lost. How many more names would be added if Fax was unable to root out the terrorist conspirators he was searching for?

Thousands, Chelsea thought, and it was enough to send her stomach up into her throat. Or maybe it'd been there for a while now, she realized, feeling nausea like an old friend, along with the relentless pound of a stress headache.

She was so far out of her element, she couldn't even see her normal life anymore. Which was why, when she reached the ME's office, she didn't go to her desk, but instead poked her head through her boss's door. "Can you cover me for the day?"

Sara looked up, her expression immediately going concerned. "Are you okay?"

"Tired, mostly," Chelsea hedged, then before Sara could ask anything else, she said, "I just got finished with Sampson."

"Him!" The word was an explosion of pent-up breath. Sara scowled. "Like there aren't enough criminals in the city that we need to go looking inside our own ranks for them? If I—" She broke off, pressing her lips together in a thin line of annoyance. "Sorry. You don't need to hear this right now."

"I just want to lie down for a while."

"You're okay to get home?"

"I'm all set," Chelsea said, letting her friend assume Seth was making the return trip, even though she was planning on catching a ride with her surveillance team. She loved her friends, and depended on them. Sometimes, though, she just needed the space inside her own head.

"Then go." Sara shooed her out the door. "Tomorrow's Saturday anyway, and I'll keep you off call. I may need you Sunday evening though, depending. The parade's going to bring out the crazies, and you know what that means."

"Busy day," Chelsea answered wanly, nodding. "I'll be here." But the parade, which had been something she'd been looking forward to only days earlier, paled when she thought about Fax and the terrorist threat to attack on—

She froze, making the connection, wondering if Fax knew about the parade yet.

"Chelsea?" Sara said. "What is it? What's wrong?"

"I've got to go." Mind racing, Chelsea rushed out of the office and found her assigned officers, and tried very, very hard not to look like a crazy person as she asked them to take her home, saying that she wasn't feeling well and needed some downtime.

She wasn't even sure why she felt like she had to hurry—Fax probably wouldn't be there until after dark either way, and she had no means to contact him and tell him to come sooner. But it suddenly seemed very important for her to be inside her own space, where he would look for her first.

When the officer pulled the cruiser up into her driveway, she would've been the first one out if she'd had a door handle in the backseat. As it was, she had to wait for the driver to let her out, and had to stay behind him as his partner checked the house. Once he'd given the all clear, she headed for her house, for her sanctuary.

She was halfway there when a shot rang out and the officer beside her crumpled and went to his knees, fumbling for his weapon.

The other cop shoved her aside and down, and went for his gun, but a second shot dropped him where he stood. Screaming, Chelsea huddled between the two of them, exposed but unable to make herself leave the fallen men.

She pressed frantically on the entrance wound in the first cop's chest while tears ran down her face and she tried to get as flat on the ground as she possibly could, knowing there had to be a third shot on the way, this one aimed at her.

Get up and run! her inner wuss screamed. *Get out of here!* But her medical training screamed louder, telling her to get in there, stay in there, keep her patients stabilized until help arrived.

Then it did.

"Goddamn it, get out of the line of fire!" Fax appeared out of nowhere, in the daylight on her front lawn, running for all he was worth, his eyes wild, his wrists lacerated and covered with blood.

He grabbed her and yanked her away from her patients just as shot number three whistled past them and nailed the corner of her house.

"No! They'll die!" She yanked away and reached back for the cops, who were bleeding out in her yard.

"So will you." Fax cursed, got her around the waist and slung her up and over his shoulder. Then he was running for the cops' cruiser, dumping her in the driver's side and shoving her over to make room.

He slammed the door, cranked the transmission and hit the gas, and they shot out of her driveway in reverse.

She lay sprawled across the bench seat, staring at her hands, which were covered in the blood of men who might not be dead yet, but would be very soon.

"Strap in," Fax ordered grimly, scooting her over to the passenger's side as he sped along the residential streets of the Bear Claw suburbs. "This is going to get bumpy."

"What?" she asked dumbly. "Why?"

He jerked his chin over his shoulder. "We've got company."

Gaping, still in shock, Chelsea looked out the back of the stolen police cruiser. Sure enough, there was a dark SUV right on their bumper.

"Down!" Fax grabbed her and dragged her head onto his lap.

Seconds later, the men in the car behind them opened fire.

Chapter Seven

Cursing a steady stream under his breath, Fax yanked the steering wheel and sent the cruiser into a controlled skid, angling them away from the gunfire as best he could while he searched frantically for an escape route.

Seeing a narrow one-lane road that claimed to lead to the highway, he thought he had it.

"Hang on!" he said to Chelsea. She braced her feet against the dash and got her seat belt on just as he overshot the turn and spun back in a cloud of burning rubber. The cruiser caromed off the curb and a street sign, and lunged onto the narrow road, where it stalled.

The dark SUV overshot, skidded, and flew into a ditch on the other side of the main road.

At Fax's shout of triumph, Chelsea straightened and looked back. Instead of whooping, she shoved at his shoulder. "Get us out of here!"

"Yes, ma'am." He cranked the engine, hit the

gas and sent the cruiser hurtling along the narrow road he'd chosen, which soon opened up to a commercial district and the highway.

Once they were on the open road, he took a long look at her, reassuring himself that the blood staining her hands and clothes had come from the cops, not her. When she looked up and their eyes met, he saw fear and shock, but no pain. "What happened to you?" she asked softly.

He glanced down at his hands on the steering wheel which were streaked with blood, and his wrists, where he'd folded his sleeves up to keep them from chafing the raw marks and cuts he'd inflicted on himself while struggling to get free of his bonds. "My cover's blown," he said succinctly, "and they know about you." He cursed under his breath, still not sure where he'd gone wrong. "I don't know what happened. I thought I'd covered myself. Maybe they got something out of Jane before she died," he mused quietly, feeling a hollow ache from knowing that Muhammad had confirmed his guess. She was gone, killed by the men he'd helped escape from prison.

She'd been one of the strongest women he'd known—hell, one of the strongest people he'd known, male or female. She'd dragged him out of depression after Abby's death; she'd given him a purpose, a reason to wake up in the morning.

She'd taught him that sometimes it was better and more effective not to care, and she'd given him a chance to make a difference, a role where the cold, unemotional shell he'd crawled behind after Abby's betrayal was an asset, not a liability.

She was the only person who'd ever really accepted him as he was rather than trying to fix him. And now she was gone.

She wouldn't appreciate his grief, he knew, but she had it anyway.

He was so wrapped up in those dark thoughts that it took a moment for him to realize the tense air in the cruiser had changed from fear to unease…and it wasn't coming from him.

"Chelsea?" he said quietly, concentrating on the road and calculating how far they could get before they'd have to pull over and switch vehicles. "What's wrong?"

Technically, the answer was "everything," because nothing was right, everything was wrong. But he knew that whatever was bothering her, it was very close to the surface. She wasn't the type to keep an important secret for long.

Sure enough, she looked over at him, her face stricken. "It's my fault."

Whatever he'd been expecting her to say, that wasn't it. "What was your fault?" he asked carefully, not liking the suspicion that immediately came to mind.

"Your cover being broken. My being shot at. The cops dying." Her voice dropped to a whisper. "I told, Fax. That's how they knew about us. I told."

Everything inside him froze to ice. "Who?"

"Seth Varitek." Her voice was very small.

"The FBI agent who oversaw the autopsy with the faked records?" he said, volume inching up in disbelief. "What the—" He broke off, throttling down the surge of rage, of betrayal, burying it beneath a layer of deathly cold. "Damn it, Chelsea."

He said nothing more, couldn't trust himself to say anything else on the subject, because once he started he might not be able to stop.

They drove in silence until he pulled off the highway into a commercial zone that included gas stations and used-car lots, along with a few restaurants. He pulled in at the back of one of the restaurants, where the overflow lot was half-full of cars.

When Chelsea glanced at him, he said tightly, "We need to ditch the car. It'll have a GPS tracker."

She nodded. "I know. And, Fax—"

"Not now," he interrupted. "I can't deal with this now." If he tried, he might say—or do—something he'd regret in the aftermath.

She sucked in a breath, but nodded. "I understand. You get us a car, and I'll strip this one of anything we can use." Glancing at him, she said, "Like a first-aid kit."

In other words, he wasn't hiding his injuries as well as he'd thought. His wrists were killing him, and he didn't want to look at his ankles, which had suffered similar abrasions and had all but stopped hurting—which he took as a potentially bad sign.

He nodded shortly. "It's a deal." He climbed out of the cruiser and strode off, looking for an unremarkable vehicle to boost.

It took him under a minute to settle on a late-nineties pickup truck with fat tires that'd work off-road and an oversize engine that ought to give it some pep across the pavement. Hopefully they wouldn't need pep or off-road capabilities, but he'd never bet on optimism before and sure as hell wasn't starting now.

He'd just gotten the engine started by cracking the column and stripping and crossing the relevant wires when Chelsea climbed in the passenger's side, carrying an armful of supplies along with her purse, which she'd managed to hang on to through the attack and subsequent flight.

She didn't look at him as she buckled up and pulled the door shut with a decisive thunk. "We good to go?"

"As good as we're going to get."

Fax backed the pickup out of its slot, hoping the owners didn't look out the restaurant window to see that they'd gained a cruiser and lost a pickup. Before he turned onto the road, though, he looked back at the cruiser and felt a twinge of guilt, not about stealing the vehicle, but because he hadn't gotten to Chelsea's house in time to prevent the officers from being killed.

"It's not your fault," she said, as though she was inside his head, following his thoughts. "It's mine."

He said nothing, because there was nothing to say, and because the world was starting to go fuzzy around the edges, warning him that he either had a mild concussion on top of the cuts and bruises, or the drugs Muhammad had used on him weren't totally clear of his system.

So he focused on driving, aiming for the airport, where the dozens of interchangeable chain hotels would offer them a decent shot at anonymity for a few hours at the very least.

"Pull in here," Chelsea said as they passed a rest stop.

"We don't need gas."

"No, but we do need cash." She lifted her purse. "I'm assuming we're not going to want to use my credit cards." Her eyes went sad, no doubt at the thought of her PD friends finding the downed officers and assuming the worst.

"Damn," Fax said, annoyed at himself. He should've pulled in at the first ATM they passed. Now anyone checking her account records would know what highway they'd jumped on.

Which went to show he wasn't functioning at top capacity. In fact, he thought as he pulled off the highway into the rest stop, he was working at about half-speed and falling.

Still, he was coherent enough to grab her wrist before she could climb out of the truck, and push the first-aid kit in her direction. "Wipe the blood off your hands, and see what you can do about your clothes."

She paled but did as he ordered, cleaning herself up as best she could before she headed into the food court to use the ATM. While he waited, Fax leaned back and closed his eyes, keeping his ears tuned for any hint of trouble.

At least that's what he'd intended to do. Instead, he dozed.

Chelsea's voice roused him from his stupor. "Slide over. I'm driving."

He shifted over, not arguing because he didn't particularly want to win. There had been no sign of the dark SUV since it'd gone off the road, and nobody else appeared to be following them.

They'd ditched the cruiser, and his gut told him it'd be a while before the switch was noticed.

They should be okay for a few hours at least, he figured as his eyes flickered closed and the dizziness took over.

It was the last thought he had for a while.

The next thing he knew, Chelsea was shaking him awake, saying, "Wake up, Fax. There's no way I can carry you. You're going to have to walk."

"I'm up." Actually, he was surprised he'd slept. Usually he could go for days on end with no rest and not feel it until he gave himself permission to let down his vigilance. Whatever Muhammad had given him, it'd packed a heck of a delayed punch.

"Come on," Chelsea said, tugging at him. "Let's get you inside."

They were in a parking lot, he saw, and noted the airplane logos on several nearby signs. "We're at the airport?" He frowned at her because he didn't think he'd said anything about going to an airport hotel, although that had been his plan.

"It was the best I could think of," she said, her voice going faintly defensive. "I switched out the truck's license plates with ones I pulled off a minivan about twenty miles from here, and registered our room under my grandmother's maiden name, figuring anyone looking for us wouldn't go that far back."

"I wasn't complaining. You did okay," he said grudgingly. He was still mad at her for leaking information, still not sure how that was going to affect things between them going forward, but at the same time he could see how it'd happened. She wasn't a trained operative, didn't live by the same rules he did.

He could understand why she'd done what she'd done, though that didn't make it the right call. Not by a long shot.

Groaning under his breath as his body echoed with pain, he dropped down from the stolen truck, careful not to lock it before he shut the door. "Let's get ourselves a room." He wasn't listening to any discussion of one versus two rooms. He didn't give a damn about modesty, and they needed to watch each other's backs.

She didn't argue. Instead, she flashed a key card and nodded to a nearby window. "First floor, halfway between two exits. That's our window. If we have to go through it, we're practically on top of the truck."

"Okay, now you're scaring me."

"Most of it's just common sense."

"Fair enough." But he didn't move, just gave her a long up-and-down look. She'd changed in the few days they'd known each other. She was bloody and battered, as she'd been in the cave that first day, but instead of being immobilized by terror, now she was functioning. More importantly, she was thinking. "You made a hell of a mistake, talking to your friend like that," he said, "but you've got good instincts. And I don't say that lightly."

She looked away. "I read lots of spy books."

"It's more than that, and you know it."

"I'm a wimp," she said softly. "I've been terrified this whole time. And my surveillance team..." Her eyes filled with tears and she crossed her arms over herself, shivering a little.

Although he knew they should get inside, out of sight, something compelled him to say, "All of this is al-Jihad's fault, first and foremost. Nothing gives him the right to do what he does."

She glanced at him and their eyes locked. He saw her searching his face for something, and wondered what she saw, what she was looking for.

"I wanted to join the FBI right out of college," she said, seemingly out of nowhere.

"Why didn't you?"

"I told you. I'm a wimp." She turned away and headed for the hotel door, apparently not willing to discuss it any further.

As Fax followed her in, she wondered how long she'd been telling herself that and why.

The hotel room was little more than a big square with two queen-size beds, an entertainment center and a small desk. Standard, unprepossessing and safe enough for the moment as far as Fax was concerned.

He locked and chained the door and made a beeline for the nearest bed, only to be pulled up short when Chelsea grabbed him and all but force-marched him into the bathroom.

"Sit." She propelled him in the direction of the toilet. "I'll get the first-aid kit."

He did as he was told, mostly because once she flipped the harsh fluorescent lights on, he could see exactly how bad his wrists looked, all gouged and swollen and so dirty they were practically a standing invite for an infection.

Staring at them without really feeling the pain, he said, "I've had worse."

"I don't doubt it," she said, coming back into the bathroom with the small plastic box she'd retrieved from the dead cops' cruiser. "But I'm a doctor. No way I'm letting you stay like this."

Perhaps, but he suspected that it was more nervous energy that kept her going as she cleaned and bandaged the cuts at his wrists. That same nervous energy rode her as she checked the bump at the back of his head and tended to the cuts on his ankles, which weren't as bad as he'd feared.

She was moving fast, talking fast, and he didn't blame her. She'd had a terrible, wretched day full of fear and blood, danger and guilt, and she had to be feeling like it'd all catch up to her if she slowed down, even for a second.

He should know. Been there, done that. He could've told her that running didn't help, though. The memories always caught up in the end.

At the same time, he knew that wasn't what she wanted or needed to hear just now, so he let her keep going, let her check his head a second and third time, get him an aspirin, draw him a glass of tap water. She needed to be doing, he knew, and maybe a piece of him needed to be done for, just for a few minutes.

He hadn't been fussed over in a long, long time.

When she was done, when she finally ran out of frenetic energy and just sort of stalled, standing there in the bathroom, staring at the bloodstains on her sleeves, he reached out and took her hand.

It was shaking.

"Come here." He tugged and she all but collapsed, practically going to her knees on the tile. He caught her on the way down, feeling the pull of bandages as he gathered her against him, her body cradled between his knees, her head against his chest. "Hold on to me for a few minutes."

She sobbed a broken word—his name, maybe—and clung.

Then, as he'd figured she would, Chelsea burst into tears.

CHELSEA HADN'T MEANT to lose it, had been trying not to, but the moment he touched her, the moment she leaned into his warm, solid bulk and felt his arms come around her, all bets were off.

She'd been trying to be brave when she wasn't really. She was a wimp who'd gone into pathology because she couldn't deal with life-or-death situations, a poser who read about adventures and imagined herself in them, but had avoided the offers of real-life adventure that'd come her way. She'd complained about her boring, normal life sometimes, but when she came right down to it, boring was better than dangerous.

"I don't want this," she said into Fax's chest, her sobs giving way to shuddering breaths. "I thought I did, but I don't. I want to wake up and realize this was all a dream. I want my old life back."

He said nothing, simply held her, and his silence was as eloquent as a shout, one that said, *There's no going back.*

She'd broken the law, broken her friends' trust, and his. And al-Jihad wanted her dead.

"What do we do now?" she said, her voice cracking on the misery of it all.

"We rest," he said, ever practical. "We're safe enough here for the moment, and neither of us is at our best. So let's rest for a few hours, and then we'll see where we're at."

She nodded, but didn't speak, and when he rose, it was the most natural thing in the world for her to rise with him, still tangled around him.

They moved into the main room together, and there was no discussion of the second bed. Instead, they lay down together, wrapped in one another, still fully clothed. He kicked off his shoes, then used his toes to shove hers off her feet. Pulling the hotel-issue coverlet over them both, he urged her into the hollow formed by the curve of his body, and his weight on the mattress. "Get some sleep. We'll overthink the rest later."

She'd slept so little the past three nights that it was easier to comply than to argue, and besides, she didn't really want to argue. She might not want to be in the situation she was in, but that didn't change the fact that she wanted to be near Fax. She wanted to touch him, taste him, curl up with him, be with him.

There would be no future with a man like him,

but foolish though it might make her, she wanted whatever the present would allow. So she cuddled up against him and laid her sore cheek against his chest. They pressed together, fitting so perfectly it made her heart ache.

The contact warmed her when she'd been so cold for too long, made her feel safe when she knew she was vulnerable. She wanted to touch him, to run her hands along his body, but she knew he was right that they needed to rest, so she let herself sink into the warmth, knowing she would be cold again all too soon come morning.

She slept, warm and secure, surfacing a few hours later, opening her eyes briefly when Fax left the bed and headed for the bathroom.

"Do I need to get up?" she asked when he returned, her voice drowsy.

"Not yet," he answered. "Go back to sleep."

The mattress dipped beneath his weight, rolling her into him. His body heat surrounded her, cocooning her in the illusion of safety. On one level, she knew she should wake up, that they needed to talk about what was happening, and what they should do next. But on another level she had no desire to do anything but sleep a little longer, put off reality for a few more hours.

So she slept.

She was awakened some time later by a sound.

Through the blinded window she could see that day had gone to dark outside, making it nearly pitch inside the room. Tensing, she strained to identify the noise that had roused her.

It hadn't been a footstep or bump in the night, she realized as her mind supplied the memory. It'd been Fax's voice.

"What's wrong?" he said from very close beside her, having apparently awakened when she did.

"You were talking in your sleep."

She waited for him to deny it. Instead, after a long pause, he said simply, "Sorry. Didn't mean to wake you."

Which meant he knew what he'd said, or at least what he'd been dreaming about. She wasn't sure whether that made it better or worse, considering that the word she'd heard had been another woman's name. *Abby.*

She didn't have any right to feel hurt. But that didn't stop the emotion from coming.

"Who is she?" she asked, not really sure she wanted to know. She'd assumed all along that a man like him was alone in the world, that there was nobody waiting for his mission to end. The way he'd talked about his mother and brothers had only reinforced that impression, as had her suspicion that he and Jane had been lovers at some point.

But none of those people had been named Abby, and he hadn't spoken of them with the intensity he'd used just now, when he'd called her name.

He was silent for so long she didn't think he was going to answer. Then, finally, he exhaled a long, sighing breath and said, "She was my wife. She miscarried and bled out five years ago next month."

"Oh." That was all Chelsea could muster at first—a single syllable that didn't begin to cover her horror, both at having asked the question and having opened an obviously unhealed wound. She could hear the pain in his voice, feel the tension in his body. "I'm sorry," she said finally, though that seemed pitifully inadequate.

"I left the PD and went undercover with Jane's team six months later," he said as though that explained everything, which she supposed it did.

"You must have loved her very much," she said, empathy warring with jealousy.

Instead of answering, he leaned away from her and snapped on one of the bedside lamps, casting the two of them in warm yellow light. He stayed there at the edge of the mattress, propped up on one elbow, looking down at her with something unfathomable in his cool eyes. "Not exactly."

The doctor in her noted that he looked less tired

than before, his eyes sharper, his color better. The woman in her, though, focused on his words. "You didn't love her?"

She wasn't sure which would be better, to hear that he'd loved and lost his wife or that he hadn't loved her, yet had married her and they'd started a family. And no matter how much Chelsea tried to tell herself this was none of her business, her heart said otherwise.

"I loved her," Fax said. "She was my high-school sweetheart. We stayed in touch while I was in the military, and got married once my service was up. I came home and joined the local PD. I worshipped the damn ground she walked on… Unfortunately, she didn't feel the same. Or maybe she did, once, but it didn't last." He paused, grimacing. "The baby wasn't mine. She didn't even tell me she was pregnant, which begs the question of whether she'd planned on abortion or figured I wasn't going to be part of her future plans."

"Oh," Chelsea said, taken aback. She'd assumed he was cold and hard because that was what his profession demanded. Now, she could only assume that his natural reserve had other layers to it, layers that made him even less available than she'd thought.

He nodded as though she'd asked the question

aloud. "Yeah. Let's just say I'm not lining up to try the happily-ever-after thing again." Something flashed at the back of his eyes and he added, "In case you were wondering."

"I wasn't," she said faintly, lying to herself as much as him. "You woke me up talking about her. That was all."

There was a great deal more and they both knew it, but instead of hashing it out, they just stayed there, staring at each other as the small circle of yellow lamplight and the night beyond cast a layer of intimacy over the scene.

Heat kindled in her belly, so much hotter than the comforting warmth of before, a greedy fire that made her want to reach out and drag him close. She wanted to sink her fingers in his hair, in his clothes, wanted to breathe him in, inhale him whole until they were bound to one another, for the duration of the night.

There was no future for them, she knew, even less hope of it than before, now that she knew his work wasn't the only reason he held himself aloof. But if she'd learned anything from the events of the past few days, it was that things could change in the blink of an eye. They could both be dead tomorrow.

Given that, there was nothing she'd rather do than rise up on her hands and knees and cross to him on the wide mattress, watch his eyes fix on her, and see the heat flare within them.

When she did exactly that, he brought his hands up to her shoulders as if in protest. But he didn't pull her close, didn't push her away.

"Chelsea," he said, voice rasping. "Be sure this is what you want."

"I'm sure enough," she said, which was the honest truth. She wasn't positive of anything anymore, but she knew if they didn't take this moment, this chance, she would regret it for the rest of her life. Now was not the time to be a wuss.

He held her away for a long moment, until she was starting to worry that her "almost" wasn't enough, that he didn't want her enough to take the chance.

Then, when she was just about ready to draw back and stammer an apology, his fingers tightened on her shoulders and he drew her close, sliding her up his body where he lay partway propped against the headrest of the motel bed.

He held her there for a few seconds, his breath whispering against her lips, his eyes searching hers for—what? She didn't know the answer, wasn't even sure of the question. But somehow he found the reply he'd been seeking, because he whispered her name, making the two syllables sound as dear as they ever had in her entire life. *"Chelsea."*

Then he framed her face in his hands and crushed his lips to hers, and there was no more talking, no more discussion. There was only the heat they made together and the perfection that might not be forever, but was exactly what both of them needed just then.

Chapter Eight

For all the times Fax had told himself to keep his hands off Chelsea, that she deserved a man who could give her all the stability and safe adventures she deserved, when it came down to it, he was the cold, greedy bastard Abby had called him in the single fight that had marked the end of their marriage and had brought on the miscarriage that had killed her.

She'd demanded a divorce out of nowhere, or at least that was how it had seemed at the time. She'd accused him of wanting everything his way, saying that he'd chosen the military, then the police force over her. She'd claimed he'd given her no choice but to have an affair, and said he couldn't blame her for going elsewhere for the love and single-minded attention he'd been unable to give her.

Well, he damn well did blame her. But that didn't mean there wasn't a kernel of truth to what she'd said.

He wanted what he wanted and did what it took to get it.

And right now, he wanted Chelsea.

She was softness in his arms, sweet flavors in his mouth and soul as he eased her down atop him and their bodies aligned. He held on to that sense of sweetness as he kissed her, trying to give her back the humanity she gave him, fighting back the beast inside him, the cold-blooded killer who took what he wanted and to hell with the world.

One kiss spun into another as he shaped her body with his hands and lips, relearning the curves of a woman, and recognizing the ones that were hers alone.

For all the times he'd sat in the hell of solitary confinement and imagined being with someone, he'd forgotten the reality of the sensations of sex, the heat of it. Or maybe he'd remembered correctly, and Chelsea wasn't like any of the other women he'd been with before.

It was a daunting thought, and one he brushed aside almost the moment it was formed, reminding himself to stay in the here and now, because there was no guarantee of tomorrow.

He tasted that knowledge on Chelsea's lips and heard it in her soft, wanting sigh. Part of him had regretted telling her about Abby, but he realized it was all for the best, because at least it put them on level footing, with understanding and expectations—or the lack thereof—on both sides.

Then she smiled against his lips and shifted to get her hands under his shirt. Splaying her fingers over his abdomen, she murmured, "You're thinking too much. I can feel it."

"I want this," he said, uttering the words before he was really aware of thinking them.

"Me, too. So why the hesitation?"

"I don't want to take advantage."

"Of?" Her eyes held a glint of humor, a hint of impatience that made his blood burn hotter, even though that should've been impossible.

He was tempted to kiss the wickedness off her face, turning the humor to heat, but he held his baser self off a little longer, saying, "You and me. Us. The situation." He gestured to the window, not at the night, but at the figment of the cops and terrorists who were looking for them even now, and would find them before too long. "We wouldn't be together like this if it weren't for some pretty extraordinary circumstances."

Her expression saddened a little. "And we won't be together after all this is over, one way or the other," she finished for him. "Don't worry, I get it."

He cupped her face in his hands and looked deep into her eyes. "Do you really? Or is this just part of some spy fantasy, an escape from what's really going on?"

But for the first time he couldn't read her every thought from her expression, leaving him off balance when she said simply, "Does it matter?"

Before he could even think to formulate an answer, she leaned in and touched her lips to his, slipping her tongue into his mouth at the same time she slid her hands beneath his waistband.

And then he pretty much stopped thinking at all.

CHELSEA FELT THE CHANGE in him, knew the second he got out of his head and into the moment, because that was when he leaned into the kiss and opened to her, deepening and intensifying caresses that only seconds earlier had seemed hotter than was possible. Before she could brace herself, buffering against too much sensation, her body flared higher and higher still, driven by his clever touch and the raw need she tasted on his lips.

Earlier she'd been the instigator, seeking to push him past his hesitation before he talked them both out of giving in to the needs of their bodies. But now he was the one doing the pushing, heating her up and over her inner barriers before she was even aware of their existence.

Always before for her, sex had been part of a relationship, an outgrowth of love. Here, though, it was all about the physical sensations, about sex rather than love. And if a small piece of her wondered whether there might be some love on her part when there was zero expectation of that on his, the heat quickly rose up and swept away the worry, leaving nothing behind except the sensation of his lips on her skin, his body against hers.

Leaving nothing but *him*.

They stretched across the bed together, twining arms and legs and tongues until there was no clear end to one of them, no clear beginning of the other. There was only them, and the heat they made together.

His skin was a tough expanse of maleness, roughened in places with faint tracks of masculine hair. Wanting more of him, needing more, she pushed his shirt aside, rucking it up under his arms until he chuckled and eased away so he could pull it off. While they were separated, he skimmed what was left of her shirt down over her arms and off, and released the catch of her bra.

Naked from the waist up and bathed in the yellow light coming from the bedside lamp, she would've blushed and covered up if it hadn't been for the look that softened his hard blue eyes—a sort of wistfulness she hadn't seen from him before.

"You're perfect," he whispered harshly. And although he was looking at her breasts when he said it, she had a feeling he was talking about more. Then he looked at his own chest, which was sharply defined with muscle and bone, and marked with a half-dozen scars of various size and ugliness, along with a ripe bruise, no doubt acquired earlier in the day. "I'm not exactly perfect," he said ruefully before looking at her once again. "Far from it." And this time she was positive he was talking about more than just their bodies.

Emotion jammed in her throat at the suspicion that he felt things far more deeply than he let on, and that he, too, knew they'd found something together that didn't come along every day.

Rather than ruin the moment with analysis, especially when she wasn't sure she was going to like the answer she came to, she lay back on the bed and smiled an invitation, offering herself to him, no strings attached. Aware that he was watching, she shimmied out of her pants and panties, leaving herself naked beneath the soft light.

She let him look, aware that he seemed to have stopped breathing as she stretched out an arm and snagged her purse off the nightstand beside the bed. From her wallet, she pulled out a condom—one of two she kept in there as part of her "just in case" stash.

Holding it up, she tilted her head and smiled at him.

"Chelsea," he breathed, only her name, but in a tone that suggested she'd just given him a gift beyond measure.

He stood then, rising from the bed to strip out of his remaining clothes. His motions were efficient and practical, like the man himself, but the play of muscle beneath his skin was an erotic dance that made Chelsea's pulse pound a greedy beat. She'd wanted him this way since the first moment their eyes had locked. She was done with waiting for the time to be right.

The time was now, right or wrong.

"Come here," she breathed, and he made short work of donning the condom over his proud, jutting flesh. Then he joined her in the center of the bed and covered her body with his.

He might've thought to prolong the moment with another kiss or some teasing caresses, but she took that inclination away by reaching up and pressing her lips to his, pouring herself into the moment and making her urgency known.

No less urgent himself, Fax kissed her long and hard as he touched her, shaping her body with his hands, sliding his fingers along her torso and hips, then inward for a long, soft rub against her center, where she was wet and wanting already.

She arched against him and cried out, her wordless plea muffled against his lips. He heard and understood, though, and shifted to poise himself at the entrance to her body.

Then he paused, waiting.

Want spiraled to a tight core within Chelsea, centered on the empty void where her inner muscles pulsed, waiting for him.

She opened her eyes and found him braced above her, looking at her. When their eyes met and the connection clicked as it had done from the first, then and only then did he nudge his hard flesh against her, into her.

His solid length invaded her, filling her and setting off an explosion of pleasure and sensation.

Chelsea gasped and arched against him, digging her fingernails into his back and reveling in his hiss and the fine tremors she could feel in his muscles.

When he was seated to the hilt he paused again and looked at her, and this time she couldn't meet his gaze, she just couldn't. The feelings he brought out in her were too huge, too raw, so she leaned up and pressed her cheek to his, closed her eyes, and hung on for the ride as he withdrew and thrust, withdrew and thrust.

The two of them surged together, racing each other to the peak while dragging one another along at the same time. The heat built and meshed within Chelsea, a building urgency in search of an outlet, concentrating at the point of contact where he filled her and withdrew, filled and withdrew.

The orgasm slammed into her unexpectedly, a freight-train hammer of pleasure and greed that gripped her, controlled her, made her arch against him and scream his name, not Fax but Jonah. She hung on to him, used his strength as an anchor while the pleasure washed over and through her. She felt him stiffen against her, inside her, and heard him give a hoarse, wordless shout. Then they were clinging together as the passion slowed and faded, leaving them limp and breathing hard, survivors of a mad rush to the finish.

And what a finish, Chelsea thought with the few brain cells left in her head unscrambled.

Where always before she'd come on a tug and roll of pleasure, this orgasm had left her flattened and defenseless, stripped bare by feelings that were too huge to deny, too important to cope with. That, and the knowledge that the two of them were a fleeting thing, a union of flesh and convenience.

The realization chilled her and made her cling to him a little too hard. She could tell it was too much because he stiffened, then he pulled away. He pressed a kiss to her cheek, but didn't look at her as he stood and headed for the bathroom, weaving slightly on unsteady legs. He shut the door behind him, leaving her utterly alone.

Feeling utterly rejected.

FAX LEANED ON THE EDGE of the sink and closed his eyes, totally undone by what had just happened between him and Chelsea.

He'd tried to hold a piece of himself back, tried to keep hold of the shell protecting himself from the outside world and vice versa, but all of his defenses had failed in that last moment, when Chelsea had grabbed on to him and let herself go, and he'd been unable to do anything but follow where she led.

"Idiot," he muttered, glaring at himself in the mirror. Worse, he'd been irresponsible, letting down his guard way too far when neither of them could afford for him to make a mistake.

Chelsea wasn't Abby, not even close. But trusting her not to cheat wasn't the same thing as trusting her to have his back. She wasn't Jane, didn't have Jane's physical or emotional tools.

Cursing, he cleaned himself up. Then, wrapping a towel around his waist in a feeble bid for the armor of clothing, he made himself leave the bathroom and face Chelsea, knowing she was likely to be beyond furious over the way he'd boogied it out of the bed they'd shared.

"Look, I'm sorry," he began the moment he hit the main room, guilt making his tone more defensive than he'd intended. "I know that probably looked pretty bad."

"It *was* bad," she agreed levelly. She was up and dressed, and had already pulled the bed more or less back to rights, as though she was trying to remove any reminder of what they'd just done. "But I'm a big girl, I can deal. We both needed some skin-on-skin after what we've been through together. Doesn't have to be any more than that."

Her voice sounded reasonable, but her shoulders were tight, her jaw was set, and a flush stained her cheeks and throat.

He wanted to tell her it hadn't been like that, at least not for him, but he stopped himself because what was the upside of explaining? It wasn't like things could go anywhere between them from here. It was probably better to have her mad at him, for both their sakes.

"Sorry," he said again, but didn't contradict anything she'd said.

"What now?"

It took him a second to realize she'd shifted gears, that she was asking about a plan, not a relationship. He was selfish enough to be relieved, wise enough to know that just because she wasn't talking about what had just happened between them, it didn't mean the issue was dead.

Or rather, it meant exactly that. Whatever might've been between them, it was over.

Guilt stung alongside another emotion he didn't really recognize, one that in another man might've been grief. Both were quickly gone as he put himself back in the agent's frame of mind he never should've let slip away.

She was right. They needed some sort of a plan.

He took a seat in the desk chair in the corner of the room, staying far from the beds, as though that would neutralize the hint of sex on the air. Thinking aloud, he said, "We know he's aiming for the parade, day after tomorrow, right? So tell me about it. You've been, right?" Hours earlier she'd identified the parade from the flyer he'd seen in the cabin.

"Sure, everyone in the city goes, pretty much." She perched on the edge of the far bed, the one they hadn't used, and frowned, thinking. "It's a local chamber of commerce thing that got picked up in the national media a few years ago during a slow news cycle. The idea took off after that, and it's become the Bear Claw equivalent of the Macy's Thanksgiving Day parade in New York. You know—floats, bands, balloons, lots of people lining the sidewalks."

Which was exactly the sort of target al-Jihad favored. During the Santa Bombings, his men had planted explosives in the highly decorated thrones of the Santas at a half-dozen malls all operated by the American Mall Corp. The charges had gone off thirty minutes after the Santas had arrived for the year, in the middle of the highly publicized kickoff parties that had been coordinated across all the locations owned by AMC.

The fatalities had numbered in the hundreds, the list of wounded topping a thousand. Even more devastating was the nature of the casualties—six Santas, along with mothers, fathers and dozens of children small enough to want to sit on Santa's lap and tell him their dreams.

It had been a truly disgusting attack, and al-Jihad was no doubt looking to improve upon it this time around.

Think, Fax told himself. *Focus.* What sort of target would appeal to the bastard during the parade? "Is there a place where there'll be a particularly large crowd?" he asked. "Lots of young kids, families, that sort of thing?"

She thought for a second, then a stricken look crossed her face. "There's an open-air party at the ski resort stadium where the parade winds up, followed by a concert and fireworks. It's the big finale."

"That'll be the target," Fax said, though it didn't play quite right in his head. The schematics he'd glimpsed in the terrorists' cabin—which had no doubt been evacuated by now—hadn't been for a stadium. Did that mean there was a second target? He didn't know and didn't have the tools or the resources he needed to figure it out.

"We need to tell someone," she said urgently. "Mayor Proudfoot will need to cancel the concert, if not the entire parade."

Fax shook his head, knowing the conversation had approximately two seconds left before it went downhill fast. "I can't. I'm sorry."

It took a moment for his meaning to penetrate, another for the anger to gather in her eyes and face. "You mean you want to *let* him attack the festival? You're going to use all those people as bait?" She must've seen the answer in his eyes, because she blew out a hollow, disbelieving breath and answered her own question. "You are, aren't you?"

He steeled himself against her disillusionment. "This business is about making tough choices."

"Choices like letting the guards, two of whom were father and son, die so you'd have a chance to uncover a plot that could kill many other people?" she challenged.

"Yeah," he said, thinking of the three innocent guards who'd been in the prison van during the escape, and the way two of the men had grabbed on to each other as they died, each trying to protect the other. *Father and son,* he thought, and could see the resemblance in his mind's eye. *Damn.*

When he'd first taken this job he wouldn't have cared as long as he reached his main objective. Now he wished he'd tried to find some way to spare the guards.

Somewhere along the line his necessary detachment had started to erode, and that was a problem. It clouded his thinking and messed up his judgment.

A prime example of exactly that was the way his heart kicked when Chelsea scowled at him. "You're not doing this, Jonah. I won't let you put the people of my city in danger."

Guilt flared alongside grief, and for a change he didn't force either of them aside. Instead, he rose to his feet and crossed to her, taking her hands. She leaned away from him, still sitting at the edge of the second bed, and he kneeled at her feet, keeping his eyes on hers, wanting, needing her to believe him when he said, "I'm sorry, Chelsea."

Her eyes filled and she shook her head. "I can't let you do this. I have to call Seth and Tucker and have them pick us up."

"I know." He slid his hand up her arm in a lover's caress that stopped at the place where her neck and shoulder joined. He said, "I'm sorry," again, and pressed his thumb against the vulnerable place where the nerves ran close to the surface.

She stiffened and collapsed.

"You really are a cold bastard, Fairfax," he told himself, feeling like hell as he raided her wallet for her remaining cash, which she wouldn't be needing where he planned to stash her. "Cold, but effective."

He wasn't feeling cold or effective as he cleared their hotel room and carried her to the truck for transport, though.

He was feeling pretty much like a bastard.

CHELSEA AWOKE in the daylight, in a different hotel room, one that was seriously run-down compared to their digs at the airport. The walls were dingy, with lighter spaces where paintings had hung. There was no TV on the bureau, although there were wires where one had been, no clock on the nightstand, none of the conveniences that usually came standard.

Panic slapped at her. Confusion.

How had she ended up in what looked like an abandoned motel, wrapped in a comforter she recognized from the airport hotel?

She remembered fighting with Fax and threatening to turn him in. After that…the panic spiraled higher as she tried to remember what'd happened next and came up blank.

Bolting up in the bed, she looked around, afraid that Muhammad had found them somehow, that Fax had been captured, too, or injured…or worse.

When she moved, there was a jangle of chain.

Terror locked within her as she looked at her right wrist. What she saw confirmed her worst fears: one end of a set of handcuffs was latched around her arm, the other on to a generous length of chain that ran beneath the bed, where it was fastened to something that didn't give in the slightest when she tugged.

She was trapped.

"Help," she whispered, her heart pounding up into her throat and choking her with terror, with tears. "Fax? Are you there?" Her voice quavered, cracking on the words.

There was no answer, no sign of him when she looked around. But there was a spare blanket folded on a chair beside the bed, and a picnic cooler on the floor beside a bucket and a roll of toilet paper. The cooler proved to contain several days' worth of food and water. A small stack of paperbacks sat on the nightstand, holding down a piece of stationary bearing the airport hotel's logo.

Pulse pumping, she reached for the note as a disturbing suspicion took root in her brain. Muhammad wouldn't have left her food, a chamber pot or a note.

Fax, on the other hand, would have.

The note read:

Chelsea, I'd say I'm sorry, but we agreed not to apologize anymore. Besides, I highly doubt an apology would suffice under the circumstances. So I'll say only that this is the best way I could think of to keep you safe while I do what I need to do.

Meeting you has been the highlight of some very dark years, and I wish it could've ended differently, but I chose my path a long time ago. You, on the other hand, still have choices left, so I'll say this: you are not a wimp, Chelsea Swan. I don't know who told you that you are, or why you believed them. I only know that you're one of the bravest women I've ever met.

It wasn't signed, but she knew it was from Fax,

just as she knew that he'd somehow knocked her out and brought her to some deserted motel, probably far outside the city and off the beaten track, figuring she'd be safely out of the way until after the parade.

Rage flared. Disbelief.

The son of a bitch had kidnapped her. Again.

Chapter Nine

Fax knew he'd done the right thing—his head and his heart both said so, damn it. He'd simultaneously protected both Chelsea and the job, buying himself room to do what needed to be done. But he couldn't help thinking that the right thing was feeling very wrong.

He'd left her as safe and comfortable as he'd been able to manage on short notice. What was more, back at the airport hotel, he'd used the business center computer to send a time-delayed e-mail that would go out to the Bear Claw PD if he didn't log on within six hours, bumping it back another six. The e-mail, addressed to her boss at the ME's office, with copies to Tucker McDermott of homicide and Seth Varitek of the FBI, gave her exact location up in the hills west of Bear Claw.

If anything happened to him, she'd be rescued within a few hours.

He'd done his best, it was true. But although he could justify it all he wanted, the end result was that not a half hour after losing himself inside Chelsea's body, he'd left her handcuffed to a cheap motel bed, with minimal provisions and a bucket.

That ranked pretty high on the bastard scale no matter how he looked at it.

"She'll be safe there," he told himself as he sent the stolen pickup hurtling back toward the city. "She'll be safe and you can concentrate on the job."

Which was true. But it didn't stop him from wishing there'd been another way. He'd spent too long in the hell of solitary confinement, and he was antisocial by nature. The next day or so was going to be torture for Chelsea, who needed to be surrounded with her friends and their chatter.

Brooding, Fax drove straight to the ski lodge where the parade would wind up the following day. His eyes were immediately drawn to a raised stadium, where crews were working to hang banners and prep for the next day's event.

The schematics definitely didn't match, but the sight of the raised seating—and the knowledge that all those seats would be filled the following day—kicked a shiver of unease through his gut, and a faint inner question of whether he might not be taking the idea of acceptable loss a little too far.

Maybe Chelsea had a point. Maybe it was time

to turn himself in and have faith that al-Jihad's coconspirators were few and far between, that the good guys would be able to mount a workable op in the time remaining, or cancel the parade and concert, at the very least.

Problem was, even if the local authorities believed him in the absence of any evidence that he was on their side, the moment al-Jihad got wind of an official response, he and the others would go deep underground, only to reappear someplace else, someplace where they weren't expected, and where there was no possibility of preventing the attack and taking down the terror-ist and his followers.

Yes, Fax was making a decision he had no official sanction to make by not warning the Bear Claw PD about the threat to the city's revelry, but he didn't see any way around it. Not if he hoped to complete his mission, which was just as vital as it had been when Jane first put him under-cover.

He needed not only al-Jihad, Muhammad and the lemming in custody, he needed to ID their connections within the FBI and elsewhere.

Anything less was failure.

When he parked at the edge of the stadium lot, he saw that there were people everywhere, both workers and early-season skiers. The lot was jammed, and there were people standing around talking, or changing into and out of their gear rather than carrying it with them to the locker room up at the resort.

Given the melee, Fax figured he was probably safe taking a look around.

He donned the black cowboy hat he'd bought at a truck stop, keeping it low so it covered his ears and brow. He slouched in his heavy jacket as he exited the truck, and consciously altered his step as he headed for the stadium, on the off chance that either law enforcement or al-Jihad's people had biometrics up and running.

There was no question that the terrorists would have surveillance of some sort. It was just a question of what kind, and how long it would take them to figure out that Fax was poking around the stadium.

He would be in and out before then. He hoped.

Making a wide circuit of the stadium first, he counted the exits and tried to figure out which structural elements would matter most to the steel-and-cement building, because they would be al-Jihad's targets.

Once he had a pretty good idea what was going on outside, he headed for a quiet-looking entrance, figuring he'd grab a hammer or clipboard and look like he had someplace to be.

He was two steps in when a blur came at him from the side.

Adrenaline zinged and Fax ducked, spinning away and then coming in low, grabbing for his attacker.

Too late, he saw a second man coming in from the other side. Cursing, Fax went for his weapon, which he'd tucked at the small of his back beneath his jacket. A heavy weight slammed into him before he got the gun and his attacker bore down on his weapon hand with a shout of "Gun!"

The second guy landed on him in a bruising scrum of knees and elbows and curses, and within ten seconds, Fax found himself kissing floor with both hands behind his back and a big guy kneeling across his kidneys.

The click of handcuffs and the burr of a police dispatcher's voice on a radio nearby let him know they weren't al-Jihad's men. Then again, so did the fact that he was still alive. It was a good bet Muhammad would've shot him on sight.

Unfortunately, just because he'd been caught by the so-called good guys, didn't mean he was out of danger.

Far from it, Fax thought, fighting to slow his pulse and think rather than giving in to the urge to struggle. He might be able to take out one of the cops, but not both. He'd have to work his way out of the situation somehow.

If he didn't, al-Jihad might very well win.

"Up you go," said the guy who'd been kneeling on Fax's kidneys. He got off and hauled Fax to his feet and started reciting the Miranda warning.

Fax got a good look at the other man, who was a tall, slick-looking guy in a pale gray suit that'd barely wrinkled in the struggle. He was wearing a nine-millimeter under his arm and an FBI badge on his belt.

There was something about him that didn't ring true. Maybe it was that his suit was high-end but his dark brown hair was overgrown past an expensive-looking cut, as though something had happened recently to put this guy off his game. Or maybe it was the look of quiet desperation in the back of his hazel eyes, one that said he wasn't totally in control of the situation.

Whatever the reason, the FBI agent gave Fax a seriously bad vibe. He'd bet money that Mr. FBI was one of al-Jihad's men.

Fax's mind raced as he tried to figure out his next best step and came up pretty much blank.

"Come on," the guy behind him said, nudging Fax's heel with his toe. "Next stop, Bear Claw PD."

Question was, would the FBI agent let him

make it that far, or was he planning on carrying out al-Jihad's kill order right away?

CHELSEA WORE HERSELF OUT struggling futilely against her bonds. She hated being stuck in the drab room, knowing that if Fax wasn't yet in jeopardy, he would be soon.

She let her head hang as tears stung her eyes. "Damn it, Jonah."

She'd begun the day making love with him. She hated that she was going to end the day cursing him. But what else could she do? She couldn't forgive the way he'd knocked her out, and the way he'd left her alone.

Worse, as the day dragged on, she started to wonder if he was coming back at all. What if Muhammad had caught up to him? What if he was already dead?

She tried to tell herself the tears that pressed at the thought were because she was afraid of being stuck indefinitely, but in reality they were partly for Fax, too. He might be the selfish bastard he saw himself as, but that didn't make him any less a hero to the people he was trying to save. And that included her.

He came off as cold and uncaring, but he'd cared enough to protect her, over and over again. And his note had gone even further. What he'd said about her being strong had mattered; it had made her consider exactly where and when she'd started thinking of herself as a wimp.

Trying to be as self-analytical as she knew how to be, she'd thought back and tracked it to her teenage years. It wasn't that her mother had called her a wimp—never that. It was more that anytime Chelsea had asked about her parents' divorce, her mother had gone on and on about how she'd tried her best to keep the marriage together and failed. She'd made Chelsea promise not to really, truly commit to a man unless she was sure he would work as hard as her to make it last.

Over the years, that had evolved into a sharp maternal pressure against failure, not just in relationships, but in everything. And so, Chelsea had realized as the shadows lengthened and the day turned to dusk, she'd started picking goals she knew she could meet, and she'd started giving up on things that seemed to come with a high probability of failure.

Like the FBI. And her love affairs.

She wasn't a wimp, she realized. She was terrified of failing.

Was that it? she wondered. Was it really so simple? What if—

The sound of tires crunching on gravel derailed that train of thought in an instant.

She whipped her head around, craning to see through the small crack between the drawn blinds and the window frame. The truck—assuming it was Fax—was out of view, leaving her to tense as she heard a car door slam.

Then another, and a third.

Panic flared, hard and hot, and she yanked at her bonds, realizing that while Fax had been trying to keep her safe by holding her in place, he'd also made her an easy target.

What if Muhammad had caught him but not killed him right away? What if he'd tortured him for her whereabouts first?

Her stomach roiled and her heart hammered up into her throat as three sets of footsteps approached the motel door. Seconds later, there was a loud slam and the door flew inward under the force of a man's kick.

Chelsea screamed, unable to stay quiet and still, unable to do anything but shriek in horror as three figures lunged through the door and bolted toward her, moving fast, their hands outstretched.

"Chelsea!" Those hands grabbed at her, tugging at her bonds. "Oh, my God, Chelsea, are you okay?"

The words penetrated, as did the identities of her attackers…or rather, her rescuers.

"Sara?" Chelsea's voice broke on surprise, and a jolt of fledgling hope. She looked from her boss to the two men who had accompanied her. Familiar, trustworthy men. "Seth? Tucker? What—" She broke off then, because it was too huge to say aloud, her surprise too great.

To her embarrassment, she started sobbing, stuttering questions and explanations that made no sense, her words tumbling over one another as her brain tried to deal with the realization that her friends had found her, that Fax had somehow let them know where to go. Which meant he wasn't coming back for her.

The thought shouldn't have hurt as much as it did.

"We've got you," Sara was saying, holding her and stroking her, and saying her name over and over while Tucker crouched down and went to work on the cuffs, quickly releasing her from her bedside imprisonment.

Seth had been the one to kick in the door, but now he stood back, watching her.

He knew something, Chelsea realized. Or else he thought he knew something and he was looking for confirmation. But what was it? Had he found out something about Fax's undercover work, or was he trying to figure out whose side she was on?

"Come on." Tucker held out a hand. "Let's get you out of here." He pulled her to her feet and Sara draped a coat over her shoulders—this one was burgundy wool and too large all over, reminding Chelsea that she'd been wearing another of Sara's coats when she and Fax first met. The memory brought a fresh burst of tears.

Get a grip on yourself, she thought fiercely, reining in the weepies through sheer force of will. *You're tougher than this.*

And, she realized with a small start of surprise, she was.

Only days earlier, she'd thought of herself as a small person capable of doing only small things, but somehow in the midst of the fear and sneaking around Fax had put her through, she'd gained a new degree of mettle.

Or so she hoped, because she was about to do something the old Chelsea never would've contemplated.

She stopped as they passed Seth. Looking the FBI agent in the eye, she said, "Where is he?"

"We have him in custody."

Nerves shimmered through her, alongside a kick of relief that at least he was alive. For the time being, anyway. "'We' as in the Bear Claw PD or the FBI?" she asked, though she wasn't sure which answer would be preferable.

"What do you know, Chelsea?" Seth asked softly, his eyes intent on hers. "And I don't mean what have you guessed or what has he told you, but what do you really know for certain?"

She hesitated, because she didn't know the FBI agent as well as some of the others, and what she did know suggested that while he was a strong personality and went his own way when necessary, he typically worked within the confines of his position. He was a company man, and she was about to ask him to work way outside the limits.

What she needed could potentially get Seth— and the rest of them—fired if it didn't work out as planned. Worse, they'd probably all go to jail.

She took a deep breath, then stepped off the deep end, into a half-baked plan that not only had the potential to fail, it probably would. But the thing was, she didn't care anymore. Fax was worth the risk. "I'll tell you everything, I promise," she said. "But first I'm going to need your help."

IT WASN'T UNTIL FAX found himself back behind bars that he realized two things: one, it was far more difficult to plan a valid-seeming escape without gadgets and outside help; and two, the only thing that'd kept him sane during his incarceration was the knowledge that someone out in the real world knew he wasn't actually a criminal.

Before, he'd been in jail because he'd chosen to be for the greater good. He'd had an excuse to feel noble and martyred.

Now, as the holding-cell door clanged shut and the guard locked him in alone, he just felt like a failure. He'd helped three deadly terrorists escape back into the world at large and hadn't been able to complete his mission.

He'd blown his cover by trusting the wrong person. He had six civilian lives on his conscience—three guards—not counting al-Jihad's accomplice—one morgue attendant and the two cops who'd been guarding Chelsea had all died as part of his botched mission. And what did he have to show for it?

Not nearly enough. He'd only identified one potential terrorist contact within federal law enforcement, and only then because the guy had come after him at the ski lodge. The agent's ID tagged him as Michael Grayson, a midlevel operative out of the Denver office, but that was all Fax knew.

Besides, he thought on an uncharacteristic beat of depression, what was the point? He didn't have anyone to report to anymore. He had to assume that Muhammad had been telling the truth and Jane was dead, her network obliterated.

Perhaps records of his undercover work still existed somewhere, but it'd be twenty to life before he'd be free to search for them, and it wasn't like he had friends on the inside ready to go to bat for him.

In the aftermath of Abby's death, he'd let those connections fall away. Some he'd even intentionally severed as part of making himself into the agent Jane had needed—one with no ties, no regrets.

No heart. The thought came out of nowhere, but it resonated more than he liked. Since when did he think things like that? Since he met Chelsea, that was when. She'd awakened something within him that had been long dormant, since Abby's death, or maybe even before that, when he'd realized the woman he'd been in love with wasn't the one he'd thought he'd married.

He'd married a fantasy. One that had looked an awful lot like Chelsea did in reality.

Sure, they were different types physically, but Chelsea had the core values he'd grown up with, the ones that lent themselves to a house in the suburbs, with a white picket fence and a couple of kids. He'd wanted that once, had thought he'd found it, only to have it disappear.

In response he'd disappeared, becoming something even his own family had turned away from. A man who thought in terms of acceptable risk and tied his lover to a bed in a boarded-up motel, and left her alone.

He was worse than a bastard. He was heartless. He was—

"There you are," a familiar male voice said, interrupting Fax's self-recrimination.

He stiffened and turned to face the man who stood alone on the other side of the holding-cell bars, wearing the uniform of a Bear Claw cop and pointing a gun in his direction.

"Muhammad," Fax said evenly. "I'm surprised you bothered to have me turn around. You're not the type to shy away from shooting a man in the back."

Al-Jihad's second in command sneered, but didn't disagree. "You're going to tell me where the woman is before you die."

"Not happening."

"You're not the only one with access to designer drugs." The terrorist tapped a code into the keypad and swung open the door to the holding cell, mute evidence that al-Jihad's reach was growing longer by the day. Now, it appeared, he had friends within the Bear Claw PD itself. Keeping his weapon trained on Fax's midsection, where a bullet might be fatal but death would be slow and agonizing, Muhammad tossed a pair of handcuffs onto the floor at Fax's feet. "Put these on. We're leaving."

Fax bent and grabbed the cuffs. Then he lunged forward, straightening as he attacked, so his head slammed into the terrorist's midsection.

It was a suicide attack, but he'd rather die now than risk giving up Chelsea's location under the influence of powerful truth-telling drugs.

Muhammad shouted and reeled backward, but stayed on his feet and brought the pistol down, slamming it into the back of Fax's head.

Fax rolled, absorbing some of the blow and deflecting the rest, but bells still chimed in his skull as he threw himself at the other man, landing a punch to the bastard's gut and then going for his throat, intending to choke the life out of him. He wanted Muhammad dead, wanted revenge on behalf of the guard's wife who'd lost both husband and son, for the morgue attendant who had been Chelsea's friend, and for the cops who'd given their lives to save hers.

Fax got a grip on Muhammad's throat and bore down, but the other man brought the gun to bear and fired.

The bullet whistled past Fax's shoulder and the report deafened him, stunning him just long enough for Muhammad to break free.

Fax reoriented, though his sense of hearing was limited to a high-pitched whine. Muhammad was on his feet, standing in the holding-cell doorway, pointing his weapon directly at Fax.

Instead of firing, he jolted, then turned and looked toward the door connecting the holding area to the main PD. Seeing something he didn't like, he spun and ran for the side exit, leaving the holding-cell door wide open.

Fax didn't waste any time. He broke for the doorway, but he was already too late. Just as he cleared the opening, a big man wearing street clothes burst through the door that led to the PD. He carried himself like a cop, and locked on Fax the moment he was through. There was another man behind him, and they looked like they meant business.

Fax didn't know if they were al-Jihad's contacts or upstanding members of the Bear Claw PD, but they were his enemies either way.

Roaring, Fax swung.

The cop dodged and shouted something, but Fax couldn't hear over the whine of temporary nerve deafness. He could only see the other man's lips moving, his eyes sparking with annoyance. Then the big guy grabbed him and his buddy got the other side and they were hustling him, not back into the cell or the PD, but toward the rear exit.

Which meant they were on the terrorists' payroll, Fax realized with a sick lurch. They were dragging him to wherever al-Jihad was holed up, and when they got him there, they'd pump him full of drugs and ask him where Chelsea was hidden.

"No!" he shouted, struggling to break free. He almost made it, only to have the guy on his right side grab a choke hold and bear down.

Gagging, Fax staggered. The first guy keyed in the code needed to get them out the back door, and waved them through, looking worried.

Fax's hearing was starting to come back online, enough for him to hear an engine revving in front of them, and men shouting behind.

Then they were through the door, and Fax froze—not at the sight of the nondescript but powerful sedan the men were dragging him toward, but at the sight of the woman sitting in the driver's seat.

Chelsea. He wasn't sure if he said her name aloud or only thought it, but it was a magic word, unlocking his limbs and brain so he could lunge forward and dive into the vehicle. The two cops piled in after him, and she hit the gas before they were all the way in, peeling away from the PD and accelerating across the city, headed for the highway.

Behind them, he imagined the other cops were too stunned to immediately pursue. They'd been betrayed by their own, by Chelsea and two strangers who had zero reason to help him.

Fax dragged himself up and onto a seat and the others did the same. He caught Chelsea glancing at him in the rearview mirror, and he said, "How did you do it?"

Her eyes went cool in the reflection. "It's called having friends, Jonah. You should try it some time."

Chapter Ten

Chelsea drove them back to the deserted motel in the silence that'd fallen after Fax's few attempts to start conversation.

"Save it until the team's all assembled," she'd snapped, trying to make it clear that he wasn't in charge anymore. At least not of her or her friends.

After Sara, Seth and Tucker had rescued her from her motel prison, she'd told them everything about her association with Fax and his claims to be an undercover fed. She'd left out the part about the sex, but could tell that Sara had guessed.

Seth, who'd heard part of it before, had interjected that he'd investigated the claim and found nothing in any of the databases that supported Fax's story, or Jane Doe's existence. However, he was willing to admit that he was no computer expert, that it was possible the files existed and he didn't know where to look, or didn't have the proper clearance.

Besides, Chelsea had argued, the very nature of Jane Doe's team meant that the records were buried deep, if they existed at all.

That was when Tucker and Seth had asked her if she really truly believed that Fax was who he said he was, and her plan was the only real way to protect Bear Claw—and the U.S.—from al-Jihad's terror network.

"I believe him," she'd said simply, and her friends had nodded and moved on from there, agreeing to help her break Fax out of the Bear Claw PD and launch their own, completely illegal, completely unsanctioned op during the following day's festival, with the intent of taking out al-Jihad and his men and flushing out the conspirators within the Bear Claw PD and the local FBI field office.

Granted, the decision had been significantly hastened by the fact that Seth hadn't much liked some of the answers he'd gotten when he'd started looking deeper at Fax's background, and noticed that his dishonorable discharge didn't mesh with his numerous commendations.

The FBI agent had been even less pleased to learn that his questions had tipped off someone who'd gotten word to al-Jihad that Fax was an undercover agent, Chelsea his contact. In fact, he'd been furious—but in Seth's case, fury apparently translated into cold efficiency.

He and Tucker had planned the jailbreak, but most of their plan hadn't been necessary because they'd gotten there on Muhammad's heels—a lucky break that Chelsea was trying not to think too hard about. What mattered was that Fax was out of the holding cell, and they were on their way to rendezvous with the rest of the group, which would include Fax and Chelsea, Seth and Tucker, along with Sara, who'd stayed behind to get a couple more of the hotel rooms ready, and Seth and Tucker's wives, Cassie and Alyssa.

Chelsea hadn't wanted to involve the other women, but Sara had been adamant about being included, and the guys had refused to shut out their wives, who were decorated cops in their own right.

That had been borderline annoying, but Chelsea had squelched the negative thoughts, knowing they came straight from jealousy. She wanted to be part of a relationship like that, formed of both partnership and love. It wasn't that she didn't want her friends to have that sort of love, either. It was just that she wanted it, too…yet had the self-destructive tendency to be attracted only to men who were completely unable to give her what she wanted.

Or maybe not, she thought on a burst of the new self-awareness she'd gained during the long, quiet day. Maybe it wasn't so much that she had bad taste in men—maybe it was that she gave up at the first sign of trouble. Maybe the long string of near misses were cases of her running away rather than putting all her effort into saving something, taking the risk that she might fail.

Well, not this time, she told herself. *I'm not giving up this time. Not on Fax or his operation.*

She glanced at him in the rearview mirror, only to find him watching her. Their eyes locked in the reflected image, and a flare of warmth kindled in her midsection.

Deliberately, she looked away and forced her eyes back on the road just as the turnoff leading to the motel came into view. They'd deal with business first. Then they'd deal with what might be the start of something important, if she was willing to fight for it, and he was willing to change for it.

Which, she acknowledged, was a big "if."

She pulled up the long, winding drive that led to the deserted motel. They'd decided to stick with the same place, on the theory that the electricity and water hadn't yet been turned off, and it offered all the concealment that had prompted Fax to choose it originally.

The closed-down motel was practically a campground, tucked into the tree line at the edge of the state park. It wasn't visible from the street and there weren't any houses for a couple of miles on either side, which meant they didn't have to worry about the lights attracting unwanted attention from locals who knew the place had gone out of business. It was a good hideout, just as it'd been a good prison.

Chelsea parked Seth's car and climbed out.

"Come on." She led the way to the room where Fax had imprisoned her, figuring there was a certain sort of irony to using the room for a strategy session.

Upon entering, she saw that Sara had gotten rid of the cuffs and chain, and the bucket. The room was back to looking like a cheap, tired motel room, with a sagging king-size bed and bare patches on the walls. The rickety desk held a pile of pizza boxes and a couple of cases of soda and sparkling water, and the cooler was now full of ice.

"All the convenience of home," Sara said wryly as Chelsea entered, but her eyes were locked on the doorway behind her.

Chelsea knew without looking that Fax had come in behind her—she could feel his presence itch along her nerve endings like fire, and she could see the anger in Sara's eyes.

Her friends might have agreed to help Fax, but

they'd done it for her sake, not his. They had, each in his or her own way, let Chelsea know they hated how he'd involved her, endangered her. Sara was even more worried, having figured out they were personally involved. Chelsea had done her best to defend Fax's decisions, but knew her friends were seriously reserving their judgment.

Stepping aside, she waved him into the room. "Fax, this is Sara."

Fax nodded. "The head ME."

"Chelsea's friend," Sara corrected with a distinct snap in her voice, and the two of them spent a few seconds measuring each other.

Outside the motel room, the rise and fall of male and female voices heralded the arrival of Alyssa and Cassie, who had stayed behind—keeping a very low profile—to see how the PD members and FBI field agents handled the incident, figuring that might give them some insight into the conspirators' identities.

Within moments, all four of them came through the door. Rock-solid Tucker and blond, tomboy-ish Alyssa were followed by dark-featured Seth in full-on brooding mode, with imp-faced, steely-eyed Cassie at his shoulder.

That meant that Chelsea suddenly found herself in a dingy motel room crowded with six other people and one pretty serious standoff, with her friends glaring at the man who had been, for one short night at least, her lover.

Sara shifted her glare to Chelsea, and she could practically see it in her friend's eyes: *Your taste in men stinks.*

"No kidding," Chelsea muttered under her breath, but moved to Fax's side. "Back off," she said. "He had a job to do, and made the choices he needed to make in order to get it done."

"But it's not done, is it?" Sara said softly. "Not even close."

"Which is where we come in," Chelsea said, although they'd already had this fight and she'd won it. "Something really bad is going to happen tomorrow if we don't stop it, and you five are the only ones I trust to help us." She turned to Fax. "I hope I won't regret this."

She half expected him to say she already should. Instead, he tilted his head in Seth's direction. "Agent Varitek?"

"Yeah," Seth allowed.

"Who did you talk to on the inside?"

Seth hesitated for a long moment, then said, "I'm not naming names right now. Suffice it to say the channels shut down way before they should have."

"Which tells me nothing."

Seth shrugged. "Sorry. That's the way it's going to be."

Fax gritted his teeth. "Then why bother to bust me out? Why not just leave me to Muhammad and his nine-millimeter?"

It was Sara who answered, "You can thank Chelsea for that."

All eyes fixed on Chelsea, including Fax's. She felt her cheeks heat and made a point of not looking at him. But he said, in a voice intended mostly for her, "Thank you."

It was a small thing that shouldn't have mattered. Because it mattered too much, she snapped, "I didn't do it for you. I did it for all the people who are going to be at that concert tomorrow."

"I'm surprised you didn't blow the whistle and have them cancel the whole thing," he said, still speaking softly, as though they weren't the center of attention.

"I was going to," she answered honestly, looking at him fully for the first time since they'd entered the motel room. "Except you were right. It's not just about the festival, and it's not even just about al-Jihad and the other escapees. We need to root out the evil, not just clip a few branches."

And oddly, the word *we* didn't seem so strange. She was involved up to her neck and she wasn't backing down this time, wasn't retreating even though the odds of success seemed very slim.

Chelsea stepped away from Fax, distancing herself from him and aligning with her friends. "You've got backup now, Jonah. Tell us what to do."

And with that, she handed him leadership of the small group, trusting him with her friends.

For a few seconds he looked as if he was going to refuse. Then his shoulders relaxed and his jaw unlocked, and something flickered across his face that might've looked like exhausted relief in another man, but on him simply looked like a moment of calm. "Thank you." This time he said it right out loud, and meant it.

"You're welcome," Seth said. "I think."

The subtext was clear—he might accept Fax as group leader for now, but they were all going to be watching him very, very closely.

"Well, I'm glad that's more or less settled," said Chelsea, deliberately breaking the tension by moving across the room and reaching for one of the pizzas. "Who's hungry?"

Fax was turning to answer her just as a set of headlights cut through the darkness. Reacting instantly, he turned the motion into a lunge, catching Chelsea around the waist and bearing her to the ground beneath him.

"Down!" Alyssa shouted, going for her weapon as the others scrambled to kill the lights and take positions.

"Stay!" Fax hissed, shoving Chelsea into the corner beneath the desk. "Don't you *dare* move." Then he was gone. Seconds later, he returned and shoved Sara in beside her, hissing the same warning.

Chelsea grabbed Sara's hands and they clung to each other while the professionals took up position around the room. She couldn't see anything—the headlights had cut out—but she could feel the incredible tension in the air, and hear a few low-voiced exchanges from the others.

Had Muhammad followed them from the PD? That was the only thing she could think had happened, unless—

A whistle sounded outside, interrupting her train of thought: several short bursts and one long, in a pattern of some sort.

The tension in the room changed, and Fax cursed—a succinct and physically impossible two-word oath.

Then he whistled back a different combination.

A third was returned.

Moments later he opened the door a crack, then all the way, and reached to flip on the exterior lights. A woman stood in the doorway opposite him, tall, gorgeous and statuesque, despite the fact that her once high-end clothes were wrinkled and stained, as though she'd been wearing them for several days under uncertain circumstances.

Chelsea scooted out from underneath the table and stood, tugging Sara with her.

It took her a moment to place the look in the woman's eyes. When she did, a chill ran the entire length of her spine and then centered in her stomach on a moment of queasiness. Her eyes looked like Fax's had when he and Chelsea had first met.

"Chelsea," Tucker said from his firing position beside the bed. "Do you know her?"

"No," Fax answered for her. "But I do." His voice had regained its cool, detached flavor, but Chelsea knew him well enough to hear the tremor of emotion beneath the words when he said, "This is Jane Doe."

"It can't be," Chelsea said stupidly as strange dread flooded her veins. "Jane Doe is dead."

"I'm harder to kill than al-Jihad and his men thought," the woman said. She looked from one to the other of the people inside the motel room, skipping over Chelsea and Sara and lingering on Seth, apparently either recognizing him from the Bureau, or instinctively knowing that he ranked within the group.

She spoke only to Fax, though, when she said, "I never saw it coming. One minute I was at my desk, the next I was waking up in a storage facility outside the city two days later. I don't know who hit me, or with what, or why they didn't just kill me outright." Her eyes hardened. "You can be sure, though, that when I figure out who it was, they'll pay."

Chelsea had to suppress a shiver at the venom in those last two words.

"How did you find us?" Seth asked. He hadn't reholstered his weapon. None of them had.

Jane jerked her chin back in the direction of her vehicle. "I had some equipment stashed for a rainy day, enough to monitor the local chatter. When I heard that Fax had turned up at the Bear Claw PD, I headed into town to see what I could do, but you'd gotten there ahead of me. When Muhammad tore off in one direction and you guys headed up here, I went with my gut and followed you." Her eyes went cool and slid in Chelsea's direction. "I hope I won't regret my choice."

Irritation prickled through Chelsea, but she didn't say anything. This was Fax's world, not hers. It was his call.

"What about the others?" Fax asked quietly.

Jane shook her head. "We were running an op a few weeks ago and it went very bad. At first it seemed unrelated, but now I have to assume that the bastard who's behind this set them up, too." She paused. "It's just the two of us now."

Chelsea didn't like the sound of that one bit, but Fax avoided meeting her eyes as he digested the new information.

After a moment he nodded. "We were just getting ready to pull together a plan." Without asking the others, he sketched out what they knew, acting as though there was no question whatsoever that she could be included.

Logically, it made sense, Chelsea knew. But that didn't stop the situation from putting her on edge. She didn't like the intrusion, didn't like the woman, especially when Jane said in a superior tone, "Of course, you realize he's targeting the stadium."

Fax nodded. "We know."

But that was another thing Chelsea had spent a good amount of time thinking about during her imprisonment. "Maybe not."

That got their attention. Fax frowned at her. "What are you talking about?"

"Remember those schematics you told me about? The ones you saw in the cabin? You said yourself they didn't look anything like the stadium or the other buildings at the ski resort. Well, I was thinking about it today, and I'm pretty sure what you described could correspond to the structures the old mining company used to cap off the played-out mines. The ski resort has reinforced them over the years and has been using them to store stuff they need out on the slopes." She paused for effect. "As of two weeks ago, the huts were stocked with equipment the engineers said the resort might need if we have another bad rainstorm and there are more landslides. That includes explosives."

She'd already discussed the theory with her friends; Cassie had actually been the one to mention the explosives. They had all agreed that Fax's description of the schematics fit with the huts. Given that the engineers were in the process of figuring out how to stabilize the slopes, which had become badly eroded in places, it seemed reasonable to suspect that al-Jihad might not be targeting the stadium itself, but rather the mountainside directly above it.

But Jane barely gave the theory a three-count before she shook her head. "No. He's targeting the stadium directly."

She turned away from Chelsea, dismissing her.

"Fax?" Chelsea said, looking right at him, willing him to back her up.

Their eyes locked. Then he looked at Jane. "The schematics I saw could be the huts she's talking about."

It wasn't exactly a ringing endorsement.

"We go with the evidence, not a 'could be,'" Jane said curtly.

"We haven't seen your evidence," Seth said levelly, coming up so he was standing shoulder to shoulder with Chelsea. The others murmured agreement and followed suit, so it was six against two.

The numbers didn't seem to bother Jane, though. She simply sniffed. "We're going after al-Jihad and his cell members at the stadium, end of discussion. Join us or don't join us, your call. But I'm warning all of you right now that if you even breathe a word of warning to anyone regarding an attack on the stadium, I'll personally see to it that you're held under the USA PATRIOT Act for as long as possible, without an arraignment or trial."

The threat hung in the air, a nasty, unfriendly thing.

Chelsea felt the heat of a flush climb her neck and touch her cheeks. She was furious with Fax for his stillness, his lack of support, his instant switch of allegiance the moment his old flame was back in the picture.

Damn him.

He looked at her now, not to make amends, but to say, "So, what's it going to be?"

She jerked her chin in the air. "We'll discuss it and get back to you."

Then, before she embarrassed the hell out of herself by crying—or screaming—in front of

Fax's gorgeous, totally in-control boss, she stalked out of the room with her friends at her back.

FAX WATCHED THEM GO and tried to tell himself he was making the right call. Somehow, though, right and wrong had gotten mixed up inside his head, blurring together until things that might've seemed very clear-cut to him before were all jammed together in an indecipherable mess.

He was seriously reeling. Within the space of three hours he'd gone from being a prisoner, to almost getting killed, escaping again, and now to being—what?

Jane's reappearance couldn't have been timed better, but maybe that was what rang faintly false.

Why and how had she shown up now? he wondered, and felt seriously disloyal for even thinking the question. Jane had saved him. She'd taught him. She was the one person he knew he could trust.

But at the same time, he didn't like the look her arrival had put in Chelsea's eyes—a mix of accusation and hurt that made him want to go to her and explain. But explain what? He owed Jane his allegiance. Surely she could understand that.

Caught in his own head, Fax waited while Jane

grabbed a slice of pepperoni and started wolfing it, as though she hadn't eaten in the more than seventy-two hours she'd been out of the loop.

Fax said, "You mentioned having some equipment with you?"

"I've got a couple of portable surveillance units in the car," she answered. "Some weapons, a couple of laptops and a decryptor that's only working about half the time." She paused, shrugging. "It's not nearly what we're used to working with, but we can make do."

She dug in to a second piece of pizza, apparently too hungry to worry about the grease on her chin when she was normally fastidious about her appearance. That was consistent with her explanation for the past few days, as was her bedraggled appearance.

And why was he even questioning it? He'd been hoping against hope that Jane would reappear and give him the bona fides he was lacking without her, the leadership she was known for. Hell, he'd wanted to see her for her own sake, and because she was one of the few constants over the past few years of his life. He should be relieved and excited, not wary.

Maybe Chelsea was right. He'd been undercover so long he'd forgotten what it meant to have friends.

"It's good to see you, Jane," he said, and meant it.

"Same goes." They shared a look and he felt something loosen in his chest, a feeling of home-coming for a man with no home.

She understood him, knew how he thought because she thought the same way. He wasn't alone anymore.

But he hadn't been alone before, had he? He'd had Chelsea at his back.

Without her, the room felt empty.

"The stadium is the logical target, but al-Jihad has to know we'll figure that out," Fax said care-fully. "What if he's doing what Chelsea sug-gested? Bringing the mountain down on the stadium could have even more of an effect than bombing it."

But Jane didn't even hesitate before she shook her head. "No, he's going to hit the stadium directly and personally. He wants to prove he can do it despite the added security the PD has put in place since his escape."

"Personally?" Fax said, surprised. "As in, he's going to be on scene?" Men like al-Jihad rarely got their hands dirty on the day-to-day workings of terror. Typically, they preferred to stay above it all and orchestrate.

"This time, yes. He's making a point." She

paused, looking at him as though trying to figure out how much to tell him. Finally she said, "I think he's trying to set up a larger group, incorporating half a dozen or so of the biggest names in the anti-American theater. This is his calling card, his show of strength."

Fax cursed bitterly. "It's part of a recruiting campaign."

She nodded. "That's what we got from the chatter we were picking up right before I was taken out." She spread her hands. "Since then I've been monitoring when I can, but I don't have anything new to add."

He took a deep breath, sorting through the possibilities. "Is there someone on the inside you can trust? Someone you can get word to who'll give us more manpower and a sanction?"

She shook her head, eyes going sad. "Three days ago I would've said yes. But I'm pretty sure the one man in the organization that I would've gone to was responsible for my abduction, and for taking out the rest of the team after the fact. It had to have been him—he was the only one who knew exactly where the team was and the sign-countersigns they were using."

"I'm sorry," Fax said, knowing that she might not show it, but the betrayal had to cut deep.

She shook her head. "It's the business." And the

thing was, she looked mad, but not hurt. As he would've been under the same circumstances a few months earlier.

"Do you know what form the attack is going to take?" he asked, forcing himself on task.

"Not precisely, but I've got a strategy mapped out." She sketched out how they could get in close to the stadium, and use one of the portable surveillance units to scan the airways and digital satellite data streams, searching for key words and flagged voices. That way, they'd be able to identify phone or radio traffic between the on-site terrorists, including al-Jihad, and his big conspirators.

Fax frowned. "Are you sure they'll be in contact with one another? Seems like needless exposure to me."

"It's all part of this big conglomerate al-Jihad is trying to set up. Trust me, the intel is solid."

And, really, that was all he needed to know. If Jane said this was the best plan, then it was the best plan, hands down.

They spent maybe another fifteen minutes discussing the details, and then wound down. By that point, Fax was sitting in the single chair with his feet up on the desk, while Jane was propped up against the headboard of the king-size bed, working on her second bottle of water.

When their discussion had trailed off to silence, she took a long pull of water, then exhaled. "I'm sorry, but I've got to ask. Is the woman going to be a problem?"

He didn't ask how or what she knew. He also didn't automatically say, *No, of course not.* Instead, he lifted a shoulder, and said, "I'm trying very hard not to let her be a distraction."

Jane arched an eyebrow. "Trying? As in, not succeeding?"

"It's complicated."

"Interesting." She looked at him long and hard, and maybe her smile went a little sad around the edges. "That's not a word you ever used to describe us, I'm betting."

"There wasn't really an 'us,' though, was there?"

"No. Not really. Which doesn't answer my original question."

"I know." He stood, draining his soda and hitting a three-pointer in the bathroom wastebasket. "You sleeping here?"

She looked around and wrinkled her nose, then stood and joined him near the door. "I'll smell like pizza if I do. I'll take something farther down."

They parted out in front of the motel; she headed for her car and retrieved a laptop, then walked to a room at the far end of the row.

Fax stood where he was, hesitating. He wanted

to talk to Chelsea, but also wanted to talk to Varitek and the others, to apologize, maybe, or see if they could find a compromise between the two groups.

He appreciated Jane's confidence, but knew her plan would benefit from additional bodies.

Jane stopped and turned near the end of the row, her body cloaked in shadows. Her voice was quiet when she said, "Problem?"

What she really meant, he knew, was *Make your choice.* He couldn't straddle the line between the two groups and be an effective agent. He needed to be clear on his priorities, and on the chain of command.

He shook his head. "No problem."

She held his eyes for a long moment before nodding. "Good to hear." Then she turned and went into her room, not looking back.

A year ago—heck, even a couple of weeks ago—he might have followed.

Now he turned the other way and headed for the woods, needing to walk off the frustration that rode him, digging greedy claws beneath his skin and warning him that what he wanted wasn't in Jane's room.

He didn't know where he was going, didn't know what drew him onward along a narrow hiking trail leading away from the motel. Using the moon to light his way, he followed the trail.

Within a short distance, the track opened up to a picnic area, a wide stone shelf that dropped away to nothing on the far side, creating a vista that was no doubt perfect for pictures and barbecues during the day. At night, though, in the moonlit darkness, it was perfect for privacy.

And romance.

Chelsea sat on one of the picnic tables with her feet on the bench and her chin in her palms, staring out into the night. She turned when she heard his approach, but said nothing, just looked at him.

She was what had drawn him out here, Fax knew. Somehow, with some sort of internal surveillance that was tuned only to her, he'd known she'd be out here. Had known there were things he needed to say to her.

Because of it, because she deserved better than what he'd given her so far, he stepped off the trail and crossed to her, stopping when he was just a few paces away.

He took a deep breath. "We should talk."

Chapter Eleven

The old Chelsea probably would've agreed in a rush, *Yes, we do need to talk. I'm glad we're on the same page.*

The woman she'd become since first meeting Fax—tougher and more aware of her own worth and ability—simply looked at him and said, "I think pretty much everything's been said, don't you?" She lifted a shoulder. "You're back in the fold. You don't need anything from me."

"That's not true." He said it so quickly that she might've thought it was a knee-jerk response, except he wasn't the sort to do or say anything without thinking it through first.

"Isn't it?" She turned away and looked back out across the vista, where moonlight hit on a canopy of pine, with occasional glints of silver tracing the path of one of the tributaries that fed into Bear Claw Creek.

She'd told herself she'd come out to the picnic

area for some privacy, but now she acknowl-edged the lie.

She'd known he would come after her. Now that he was there, though, she didn't know what came next.

After a moment, he hitched himself up and sat beside her. "You're wrong. I do need you."

The words sounded like they came hard to him, but she had little sympathy. "You cuffed me to a bed and left me alone because I threatened to go to the cops. Let's face it, that's not the sort of thing a guy does if he's looking for a long-term relationship."

A muscle pulsed at the corner of his jaw. "I did what I had to do."

"You did what came easy to you."

"It wasn't easy." His words were low and intense, and he surprised her by taking her hand in his, and threading their fingers together. "I won't apologize, because I'm not sorry. But I will say that it bothered me more than I'd expected it to."

"Because you'd spent so much time in solitary confinement," she said, trying not to feel the way their palms matched up just right, or the fine shimmer of warmth that trailed up her arm from the simple contact.

"Because I was leaving you behind."

The simple statement sliced through her, leveling her carefully built defenses. She floundered for a few seconds before saying, "I don't know how I'm supposed to feel about that."

"Me either." He moved a little closer to her on the picnic table and laid their joined hands on his muscular thigh. They were touching at hip and shoulder now, and she had to force herself not to lean into him as he continued, "I wasn't looking for anyone, you know. I don't have room in my life for a friend, never mind a lover."

"You slept with Jane." She hadn't meant to go there, but how could she not? She might've suspected the relationship before, but the moment she'd seen them together she'd known for certain. It was in the way they'd looked at each other, the way they'd leaned close to talk, well within each other's space.

"We had mutually agreeable sex. That doesn't make her my lover."

She winced. "That's cold."

"This isn't." He lifted their joined hands and pressed his lips to her knuckles, sending a frisson of heat radiating through her. "This is different, whether I want it to be or not." He paused, then admitted, "I hated leaving you here, but I didn't know what else to do. It wasn't about you calling the cops, either. Not really."

She didn't want to ask, didn't want to let him weaken her. But the feel of his body against hers and the good pressure of their fingers intertwined had her saying, "What was it about?"

"I was afraid." He said the word like it was a curse. "When I saw your police detail go down and I knew Muhammad and the others were out there, gunning for you, I couldn't handle it. I was scared and furious, and I couldn't get to you fast enough."

His voice was so raw, the emotion etched so clearly on his face in the moonlight, that her heart turned over in her chest. She squeezed her fingers on his. "You did get to me. You got me out of there, kept me safe. I'm fine."

"You might not be the next time. These guys are killers, Chelsea. If they want you dead, you might as well already be in the meat wagon."

Her blood heated, not just at his words, but at the emotion beneath them, which was more than she'd expected, more even than she'd hoped for on the few brief occasions she'd allowed herself to hope.

Which didn't change the way his face had lit when he'd seen Jane in the doorway, or the way the two of them had leaned close together, shutting the others out, including her.

"Why are you here, Jonah?" she said quietly, wishing he would go away, because if he didn't she was likely to do something she'd regret.

He didn't pretend to misunderstand. "Damned if I know."

"You should be with Jane."

"What if I'd rather be with you?"

"Can you honestly say that?"

His silence was answer enough, and Chelsea felt something wither and die within her. She pulled her hand away from his and stood. "I didn't think so." She turned to face him, her throat tightening a little at the moonlit sight of the man who had become too important to her in too short a time. "Let's not make this any harder than it already is, okay?"

She didn't really expect an answer, didn't get one. A moment of silence drew out as they stared at each other, knowing there really wasn't any answer to the gulf separating them—one of experience and priority, of lifestyle and goals.

Then she turned away, her eyes filling with angry tears as she returned to her room alone, leaving him in the darkness.

SHE WAS RIGHT, damn it. Fax knew it, knew he should leave things well enough alone. They'd had their moment and it'd been a good one, but neither of them had thought going in that it was going to be more than a flash in the pan, a night or two in the midst of chaos. He wasn't the sort of guy for more than that.

So why did he feel like kicking the crap out of

the picnic table and howling at the moon? Why did he want to follow her and pick a fight, argue the impossible?

"You were in prison, idiot," he muttered as he dragged himself off the picnic table and headed back toward the scattered lights coming from the motel. "You were bound to get hooked on the first woman you saw."

Which sounded logical enough. Too bad he couldn't convince himself it was the truth. He'd gone longer between lovers before. Hell, after Abby died, it'd been more than two years before he'd taken Jane up on her no-strings offer, and they'd only been together maybe a dozen times total, and then only when it made sense.

He and Chelsea made no sense whatsoever. Yet damned if he didn't hesitate when he reached the front of the motel, knowing he should get some sleep in his own drab room, but wanting to knock on Chelsea's door instead.

Let's not make this any harder than it already is, she'd said, and he knew she was right. Thing was, he wasn't sure he wanted to take the easy way out this time.

"Looking for company?"

He turned at the question, feeling a complicated mix of emotions at the sight of the woman backlit in her motel-room doorway.

The wrong woman.

He summoned a smile for Jane, one that felt like respect and trust, and nothing more. "Hey."

"I'll take that as a 'no.'" She didn't look like it bothered her one way or the other, but her expression hardened as she approached him.

She was wearing a T-shirt and yoga pants, no doubt borrowed—or more likely commandeered—from one of the other women. Even in the casual clothes, she looked like a leader, like a warrior in the battle against terrorism.

Tilting her head, she looked at him long and hard, then said simply, "You'll want some time off after this, to make your decision."

"I made my call a long time ago." Or rather, circumstances had made it for him. Maybe back then he could've gone in a different direction, made a different choice, but he'd seen and done too much in the intervening years.

He couldn't go back to real life now. He could only protect it for others.

"Are you sure? If your head's not in the game…" She let the sentence trail off, but he had no trouble filling in the blank. If he wasn't for her he was against her, and she'd leave him behind rather than let him interfere because of conflicted loyalties.

He knew, because it was what he would've

done in her shoes. At least it would've been a few weeks earlier. Now, he couldn't be entirely sure what he would've done in her place. He only knew that he damn well needed to be in on al-Jihad's takedown—not just because he'd spent the past two years working toward it, but because the bastard was after Chelsea and her friends, and the residents of Bear Claw.

He couldn't give Chelsea the commitment and the caring that she needed, but he could damn well protect her, and the people she cared about.

"I'm so far into the game it's not even funny," he grated, letting Jane see the determination in his eyes, and an edge of threat. He was in this one whether he went with her or through her. It was her choice.

Her lips curved ever so slightly and she nodded. "That's what I wanted to hear." She turned and headed back to her room, but paused at the threshold and looked back. "You've always been my best. After this, we'll rebuild, and you'll be in it every step of the way. Two teams—one mine, one yours. You have my word."

His own team. It was an honor, a promotion. And it would consume his every waking moment from there on out.

Fax nodded. "I'm flattered."

"And?"

"I'm in."

"Good." She didn't say another word, just headed into her room and shut the door at her back.

Fax just stood there for a moment. Then he said, "You heard that, I take it?"

Three rooms down, Chelsea's door opened from the cracked position it'd been occupying. She stood framed in the doorway as he crossed to her, trying to read her expression and failing.

Wearing bike shorts and a plain T-shirt, she should've looked soft and vulnerable. Instead, she looked supremely self-contained as she tilted her head and said, "I heard."

"And?"

"What exactly is it that you want me to say?" Her eyes glittered, but with temper, not tears. "Congratulations?"

"Say you understand," he said, the words coming from nowhere, from somewhere deep inside him, emerging before he knew he was going to ask.

She smiled with zero humor. "I understand that leading a team will be far easier—and way more comfortable—for you than trying to make a change."

Anger flared, more familiar than the nerves that shimmered too near the surface. "That's low."

She lifted a shoulder. "Truth hurts. You didn't—

still don't—want to trust me or my friends, because that might've proved that the way you live your life isn't the way it has to be, that you've got other options if you'd only be brave enough to reach out and grab for them."

"I'm not the one who thinks of myself as a wimp."

"Neither do I. Not anymore. No," she said softly, her focus turning inward, "I've given up too many times because I was afraid to try something I might not succeed at. But not anymore. I'm done wimping out."

"Is that what this is about?" he snapped. "Leading your friends up the mountain on the basis of zero evidence isn't exactly going to prove that you're brave. Seems to me you're heading away from the fight."

"You're getting nasty. That means you know I'm right."

He stepped closer, until he was in her space, crowding her, breathing the same air she was. "It means I'm getting annoyed with this conversation. What exactly do you want from me right now, Chelsea? Another apology?"

"No. I want you to come inside." She stepped back, into the motel room where he'd left her cuffed that morning, thinking it might be the last time he saw her.

She'd been unconscious, her eyelashes lying on her pale cheeks, her lips curved faintly on some dream he could only guess at, and envy.

His brain locked on the memory and on the invitation.

"You want…" He trailed off, sure he'd misheard.

But she crooked a finger. "I want you. Inside. Now."

His feet moved before he knew he'd made the decision, propelling him into her motel room. His hands worked of their own volition, closing and locking the door, and putting the pitiful chain in place. But before he could touch her, he forced himself to stop, forced himself to be sure this was what she wanted.

He lifted a hand and brushed a strand of hair away from her mouth, in a gesture of tenderness that felt both foreign and right. "I can't be what you need."

She raised an eyebrow. "You think I haven't figured that out? Please." But she caught his hand in hers, and pressed his palm to her cheek. "This is it, Jonah. It's been a hell of a week, but as of tomorrow, it's over. Back to real life for me, back to the shadows for you. This is our last night. I'd rather not waste it being mad at each other for things we can't or won't change."

He knew he should do something, say something; knew he should either move in or away from her, but he couldn't do a damn thing. He didn't trust himself to get it right, didn't trust himself not to hurt her in taking what he wanted more than he wanted his next breath.

He'd nearly talked himself into being the gentleman when she leaned up on her toes and touched her lips to his.

And he was lost.

CHELSEA KNEW she was making a big mistake, but she had to believe it'd be a bigger mistake to let him walk away without taking what she could get of the magic they made together. If it was just sex, then that was all it would be. And if, deep down inside, she knew it was far more than that on her part, she'd deal with that heartache tomorrow.

Tonight she wanted the man, *her* man, for this one final night they had together. So she kissed him, and was prepared to hang on tight if he tried to pull away.

She wasn't prepared for him to kiss her back. Which was exactly what he did, grabbing on to her and leaning in hard, taking her kiss from an invitation to a demand in the space of a second.

Heat speared through her. Want. Longing. And raw, no-holds-barred lust.

Whereas the night before had at least been cloaked with the illusion of romance, now there was none. He bent her over his arm, ravaging her lips and throat, his grip on her so tight she could do little more than sag back and moan with the feel of him, and the heat that spiraled up within her.

He bore her to the bed where he'd chained her that morning. Chelsea had a brief flash of wishing Sara hadn't disposed of the cuffs, followed by a hard blush brought on by the thought.

Fax's rusty chuckle let her know he'd read her expression, or else his mind had paralleled hers. She opened her eyes to find his face very near hers, his eyes gone flinty with passion.

He was breathing hard, with quick rasps—they both were. They were twined together on the yielding surface of the mattress, although she wasn't sure when they'd gotten there or how. Her T-shirt was up around her throat, and his hands were on her breasts, chafing them, working them until her entire body was a coil of sensation.

She arched back and cried out, dragging at his clothes, at his hard body atop hers, needing more, demanding more.

They parted only long enough to shed clothes and pull aside the cheap bedspread he'd stolen from the airport hotel, and for him to don the second and last of the condoms she kept in her purse. Then they were back on the bed straining together, chasing each other through the flames that licked around her, inside her.

He thrust into her without preamble, a tremendous surge that had her biting back a cry. He buried his own shout in her mouth, both of them aware that they weren't alone at the motel, yet at the same time unaware of anything but the slide and slap of flesh and the raw need that drove them together and apart, together and apart.

She came fast and hard, clamping around him, vising her calves behind his hips and driving him deeper and deeper still. He plunged into her again and again, spurring her onward, prolonging the pleasure until it passed beyond her comfort zone to something that wrenched her gut and warned that she would never be the same, she would never have another lover who could measure up to what she had experienced with Fax.

Then he cut loose, going rigid against her and muffling a long, hollow cry against her throat. She felt him pulsing within her, felt the long, drawn-out shudders that wracked his big, strong body, and she wrapped herself around him, giving herself to the moment, to the man, as she came again.

Tears tracked from the corners of her eyes and

mingled with the sweat that prickled her body and then cooled, binding them together as surely as their flesh was united.

She'd been lying from the start. It hadn't just been sex for her. Not by a long shot.

Fax shuddered one last time and went limp against her. He looped his arms around her waist and hung on like he never meant to let go, and she allowed it because she was helpless to do otherwise, helpless to stop another tear from building and breaking free.

"Crushing you," he muttered thickly, and rolled to his side, taking her with him, rearranging them so they were spooned together, her back to his front. Then he pulled the coverlet over them both. He murmured something else, low and sweet, and too slurred for her to understand.

Within minutes, he was asleep.

Chelsea, on the other hand, was wide awake. She knew what she had to do and hated it. She wanted to stay in his arms, wanted to draw out every last precious second they had left together. But, really, their time had already run out. She was already using borrowed hours, time stolen from the people who trusted her, who needed her.

Slipping out from underneath Fax's sleep-heavy arm, she rose from the bed. Forcing herself not to look back, not to regret, she got dressed in her jeans and heavy shirt, and carried her shoes to the door.

There, she did look back. And immediately wished she hadn't.

Fax looked fierce even in his sleep. He'd pulled her pillow to his chest, cradling it as though he was still trying to protect her, trying to keep her close. Only, he'd protected her well enough, but he'd never let her close, never let her inside.

And after what she was about to do, he never would.

"Now it's my turn to say I'm sorry," she said, hanging on to the door frame to keep herself from going back to the bed and touching him, kissing him the way she wanted to—the way that would be guaranteed to wake him, guaranteed to give him a chance to stop her. Which wasn't an option. So instead she touched her fingers to her sex-swollen lips and blew him a kiss. "Goodbye, Jonah."

She closed the door quietly behind her, and tiptoed away from Jane's room. The other woman couldn't know what they planned.

At her quiet knock, Seth opened the door to the room he and Cassie were sharing. He was dressed for action, and the others were gathered at his back. "Thought you weren't going to make it," he said, his eyes narrowing on hers.

"I'm here now," she said, refusing to explain, or make excuses. "Let's go."

A KNOCK ON THE DOOR roused Fax an hour past dawn. He was alone.

More than that, the sheets beside him were cool to the touch, and something inside him said that Chelsea had been gone for a while.

She went for breakfast, he told himself, knowing it was a lie and hating the dismay that shot through him, the worry.

After yanking on his pants and shirt, he opened the door. He was unsurprised to see Jane on the other side, and equally unsurprised to see that she was alone. "They're gone," he said. It wasn't a question.

Jane nodded. "Around 2:00 a.m."

Fax stiffened. "You heard and didn't stop them? Didn't come get me?"

"What would you have done?" Faint scorn laced her voice. "Get your head out of your pants and into the game, Jonah. If they're not fully on board with the plan then we're better off without them."

"What if they go to the cops?"

"They won't. They bought into that much of it." She jerked her chin in the direction of the mountain. "They're on their way up there, which is just as well for us. It'll get them out of our way while we do the real dirty work."

She held his gaze, awaiting a response.

But what could he say? She was his boss. She'd saved his life and been what he'd needed, when he'd needed it. Chelsea and the others were… Damn it, he didn't know what they were anymore.

Chelsea had gotten to him in a way no other woman had since Abby. Hell, his feelings for her made the feelings he'd had for Abby look like a cheap imitation of lust and caring and—no, he wouldn't call it love, couldn't use a word like that, when he knew damn well it'd be a lie.

"Your call, Jonah," Jane said. But they both knew he'd made his choice long ago and had re-affirmed it just the night before. He was her man in all the ways that really counted.

He jerked his head toward her vehicle. "Let's go. Two of us will be enough."

It would have to be or Bear Claw was in serious trouble.

He'd deal with Chelsea's defection later. Or maybe not. Maybe he'd just leave town. It might be easier for both of them that way.

Chapter Twelve

By 9:00 a.m. Sunday, Chelsea and the others were in place.

They split up: Sara went with Tucker and Alyssa, while Chelsea stayed with Cassie and Seth. They hid off to the side of the main fault line, one group for each of the two mine-top huts they believed would be al-Jihad's target.

The huts were low steel structures built into the side of the mountain. More importantly, they flanked a hundred-foot-wide swath of unstable mountainside, which had been weakened by mining efforts and seriously destabilized by the recent rains.

Although the engineers swore it would stay put until they got their terracing and trenches in place, allowing them to trigger a so-called controllable avalanche, it looked precarious to Chelsea, and the cluster of buildings making up the ski lodge, which she could see at the base of the mountain, looked very small in comparison.

The idea of someone bringing the mountain-side down on the stadium was enough to have her stomach in knots, but she breathed through it, knowing they were there to prevent exactly that.

Since cell transmissions could be detected, they'd agreed on a simple system of whistles and birdcalls to communicate.

The stealth proved unnecessary, though, as nine o'clock turned to ten, then eleven with no sign of company. The six friends were alone on the mountainside, and the parade had to be past the halfway point by now. There should be some activity if this was truly the terrorists' target.

Either they'd guessed wrong or there'd been a change in plans.

As she waited, Chelsea tried to keep herself from imagining how Fax must've felt when he woke up and found her gone, found all of them gone. She told herself it served him right for chaining her to the bed—fair was fair. But no matter how hard she tried to be, she wasn't the vindictive sort. If there'd been another way to do what she felt she needed to do, without going behind his back, she would've.

Unfortunately, he'd made his loyalties all too clear, and Jane had come out on top of that particular battle.

Sorrow and anger mixed inside her, reminding her of what she'd walked away from. Or rather, what he'd chased her away from. Because he'd made it crystal clear: he didn't want her enough to change.

Well, guess what? She'd already changed and she didn't intend to backpedal and return to the woman she'd been before. If he couldn't handle the person she was becoming, he didn't deserve her.

But even though he'd told her himself that he didn't deserve someone like her, she couldn't help thinking their main issue wasn't what she did or didn't deserve; it was whether he wanted what they'd had together enough to make the change… and the answer was a resounding "no."

Damn him, she thought, checking the time and wincing when she saw it was quarter to twelve.

"This is no good," Cassie said quietly. "Maybe we should consider heading down the mountain and hooking up with Fax and his—" She broke off with a glance at Chelsea and finished with, "boss."

Which so wasn't what she'd been thinking.

"They won't have us at this point," Chelsea said quietly. "She's probably already leaked a hint that we might show up there. The second we make an appearance, we'll be guests in our own jail."

Or rather, what had been their jail before they'd gone renegade. Chelsea didn't regret making the call for herself, but she was seriously wondering if she'd torpedoed her friends' careers based on nothing but her own insistence that Fax wasn't like the others.

Only he was, wasn't he?

"Hey." Cassie touched Chelsea's arm, giving it a squeeze. That meant more than it might've otherwise, because Cassie wasn't the touchy-feely type. "This isn't your fault. If it were easy to anticipate what this bastard was going to do, he wouldn't have gotten away with half the stuff he's accused of, and he would've been in a cage long before this."

"And he would've stayed there," Seth agreed.

"We should've listened to Jane." Chelsea's shoulders slumped. "I was trying to prove a point and it backfired." She'd wanted to make Fax take her side. Instead, she'd split their forces.

If she didn't fix the mistake fast, there was a good chance that innocent people were going to die. And she did *not* believe in acceptable levels of collateral damage.

In her world, one unnatural death was one too many.

"I'm going to take a look around," she announced, rising to a crouch that kept her below tree level in the undergrowth beside the low Quonset hut. "If the coast is clear, I think we should go down the mountain."

"Keep your head low," Seth said, but he didn't tell her not to go, which she took as proof that he also thought they were in the wrong place.

"Count on it." She worked her way out of the thicket, walking along the faint brush marks they'd left in obscuring their trail. They'd tested each step carefully to make sure they didn't wander onto unsafe ground, so she knew if she followed the marks she ought to be okay.

She kept careful watch, but saw only mud, stones and uprooted trees thrown around by the last big slide. There was no sign of anybody else on the mountain, no sign that al-Jihad and his men had ever considered attacking the site.

"Damn," she muttered, though she wasn't sure why she'd thought there might be something, some indication that—

The blur came at her from the side, a whistle of motion and a thump of impact that spun her and drove her staggering back.

Panic came hard and hot, and she screamed at the sight of Muhammad's face, the murderous satisfaction in his eyes.

Then there was another thump, and the world went dark.

FAX HAD A BAD FEELING about the setup at the stadium. It smelled wrong to him, felt wrong. If he'd been alone, he would've banged a U-turn halfway there and headed up into the mountains. Or maybe he would've kept going, figuring the others could handle whatever his gut told him was up there, while he needed to deal with the situation at the stadium.

The danger was up the mountain and in the stadium, and inside his own skull, buzzing and tugging at him, and making him crazy.

Or was that the woman making him nuts? Was it Chelsea and the way she'd seduced him, exhausted him to the point that he hadn't noticed the six of them leave the motel?

Part of him was furious at her deception. Another part of him was a little impressed. Not that he'd ever tell her that. Not that he'd ever get the chance to tell her.

Jane drove fast, weaving in and amongst the traffic as the parade ended and the crowds geared up for the concert. Her jaw was set, her eyes locked on the road with the single-minded determination that'd made her the best of the best and that had drawn the two of them to one another.

They'd been good together because they'd been the same. Still were.

When that rang faintly false and bumped up against the churn in his stomach that said they were headed the wrong way, he tamped down both sensations and checked his weapon for the fifth time since he'd gotten into the car.

"You're fidgeting," Jane said without looking at him.

"I'm fine."

"If you say so."

They didn't speak again until she'd pulled into a spot at the stadium. They each got out of the car, and Fax took a good, long look at the horseshoe-shaped rows of stadium benches, which rose high into the mountain air. He muttered a curse and then said, "What are we thinking? We couldn't cover this place on our own if we had two dozen highly trained operatives. And where is the surveillance equipment?" He turned toward Jane, saying, "I thought—"

"Fax," Jane interrupted, her voice tight.

He turned and froze in place at the sight of the man standing beside her, sharp-featured and weasely. Lee Mawadi.

Fax's blood iced in his veins. The bastard had Jane by the arm, and was holding a gun to her side, its muzzle pressed into her waist. He had the stones to smirk. "Not as smart as you think you are, huh, Fairfax?" He dug the weapon in harder, wringing a cry from Jane as he grated, "Toss your weapons back in the car. And don't try anything or the bitch here gets a few new holes."

Fax did as he was told as killing rage speared through him. He two-fingered the gun, then tossed it in the passenger's-side footwell.

"Now who's the lemming?" Lee jeered.

Fax didn't reply, didn't get a chance to, because suddenly the bastard was letting go of Jane and turning the weapon on Fax, and Jane wasn't doing a damned thing except standing there. Watching.

In a second of ice-cold reality, Fax understood what his gut had been trying to tell him since the night before, the instinct he'd ignored because he'd thought it was a mixture of lust and guilt.

Jane's reappearance had seemed too convenient because it *was* too convenient. She'd been working for al-Jihad all along.

Which meant Fax had, too. Maybe not all along, but for a while, at least.

Hell, he'd probably gone to jail for the bastard.

How could you? he wanted to ask her, but he could tell from her stone-set expression that she wouldn't answer, didn't care what he thought of her, didn't give a single damn about him.

She'd never claimed to care about anything but taking down al-Jihad and even that had been a lie.

"Steady, Jonah," she said, waving for Lee to lower his weapon. "Think it through. Think of the advantages."

"I'm way ahead of you." He smiled mirthlessly,

cooling his expression even though his blood was quickly heating once again with anger, with panic.

Jane had known the others were headed up into the mountain.

For all he knew, they were already dead.

Jane's face softened with a hint of approval. "You already knew about my change in allegiance."

"I guessed," he said. "Good to know the time in prison hasn't dulled my instincts too much."

"He's lying," Lee hissed, bringing his weapon up once again. "He never would've sent the bitch to Muhammad. He's too much of a goddamn prince for that."

"And you're too much of a rodent to understand the concept of developing an asset for future use, then disposing of it when it ceases to be useful." Fax forced a smile, although his stomach roiled as he said, "Trust me, she came in *very* useful for a while."

That startled a chuckle out of Lee, who let the gun drop a notch.

It was all the opportunity Fax needed.

Moving fast, he lunged for the weapon, grabbing Lee at the same time that he swung a kick in Jane's direction, forcing her to stumble back, out of range. He fought with Lee, kicking and punching as the smaller man squirmed to get free and struggled to bring the gun to bear.

"You don't want to do this, Jonah," Jane said, her voice edged with irritation or maybe fear. "Don't be stupid."

"No." Grunting with the effort, he yanked the gun away from Lee and subdued the bastard with a choke hold. When Jane came at him, he dodged and grabbed her, and whipped her arm up behind her back as well. "I've been stupid for way too long already."

Using the gun to keep them pinned down, he yanked off Lee's belt and used it to bind their hands together at the smalls of their backs.

Then he turned toward the stadium, pointed the nine-millimeter in the air, and fired off four rounds in quick succession.

Screams and shouts erupted, and the people who'd been streaming into the arena only seconds earlier started scrambling to get out. Already set on a hair trigger after the prison break, the citizens of Bear Claw didn't wait to see where the shots were coming from or where they were aimed.

They bolted en masse, creating instant chaos.

Satisfied, Fax returned his attention to his two prisoners. He was just in time to duck the full-power kick Jane had aimed at his privates. Her foot struck him a glancing blow in the groin that sent a slash of pain through him and had him staggering.

They'd gotten free somehow, and Lee was

already running. Jane paused and grabbed Fax's gun from the passenger's seat of her car.

She came up firing and she wasn't aiming into the air.

Fax hit the deck and rolled partway under the car, then scrambled up again. There were more screams, more chaos, and cars started peeling out of the parking lot. By the time Fax was up and oriented, Jane and Lee were both gone. Not good.

On the upside, though, the stadium was more than half empty, and—

An explosion roared from the main entrance, slamming him to the ground.

He heard more screams, dulled now by the ringing in his ears, then the thump of more explosions, the squeal of tires and the crashing impacts as cars collided, starting a chain reaction of accidents, with cars accordioning into each other in the drivers' mad rush to get the hell away from the bombs.

Which meant nobody was going anywhere, Fax realized as he levered himself up and took in the scene.

The stadium was wreathed in ugly gouts of black smoke that rose from each of the collapsed entrances. There were thousands of people still trapped inside and probably the same number stranded outside in the parking lot and road beyond, which had become impassable due to wrecked vehicles.

In the distance, he could hear sirens and emergency vehicles approaching, but it'd take too long for them to fight through the jammed roads. In the meantime, thousands of people would remain trapped in the bowl-shaped depression where the stadium had been built at the base of the mountain…right below the threatening shelf of a potential landslide.

Chelsea and the others were up there, Fax thought, his heart hammering painfully against his ribs. For all he knew, they were already dead, killed by al-Jihad and his ruthless terrorists as they cleared the way for the next stage of the plan.

It wasn't a case of the landslide or the stadium: the bastard had targeted both.

"I should've seen it," Fax said, cursing himself as he fought through the mob, headed for the road below, which was rapidly jamming with cars. "I should've known."

But he didn't, he hadn't. And because he hadn't been thinking clearly, innocent people that he cared about—yes, *cared,* damn it—might already be dead.

He hurled himself down the steep incline to the road, his feet barely moving fast enough to keep up with his momentum. He staggered when he reached the level strip of grass beside the road, but righted himself and kept running until he found what he was looking for.

The red SUV was empty, parked in the farthest lane with the driver's-side door open and the motor running. No doubt the driver was one of the many people who'd gathered at the edge of the road, shading their eyes and staring up toward the smoking stadium, talking in high, excited voices.

Fax climbed in the driver's seat and slammed the door, then hit the button to lock the vehicle tight. He was most of the way out of the nose-to-tail line of cars when a man ran at him, waving his hands and shouting.

Fax cracked the window and shouted, "Police business. You'll get it back."

Then he hit the gas and sent the SUV hurtling across a strip of grass and into the wide ditch separating the eastbound and westbound lanes of traffic. The SUV dug in and bounced hard and its tires spun. For a second, Fax was afraid the thing was going to dig itself into place and he'd be stuck. Then it tore free with a roar and a lurch, and started climbing up the other side.

He didn't wait for a break in the rubbernecking traffic in the other lane. He just hit the gas and aimed for a gap that wasn't quite big enough for the SUV. Paint scraped and the vehicle shuddered and bounced as he fought it into a straight line following the road.

Nearby drivers swerved, honked and swore at him, but he didn't care. He leaned on the horn and flashed the high beams like a crazy man, and weaved in and out of the near-gridlocked traffic.

The other drivers must've thought he was with the emergency rescue personnel or something, because they started getting out of his way, just a few at first but then more and more of them, opening up a pathway until he was free, on the open road headed for the turnoff that would lead him up the mountain.

Once he was speeding along and not focused solely on the driving anymore, his brain kicked back online, and all he could picture was Chelsea's face as she'd slept, all he could imagine was that same face, still and gray, with her stretched out on a table in her own morgue, dead because he hadn't listened to her, hadn't trusted her, or his own instincts.

"No," he said aloud, denying the image, denying all of it. He would be in time to get to her, would be in time to save her.

Failure was *not* an option.

Chapter Thirteen

When Chelsea regained consciousness, it took a few moments for her eyes to clear and her brain to process what she was seeing. Memory returned with a brutal slap when she saw dirt, ledge stone and uprooted trees all piled in a disarray, tilted at a seemingly impossible angle.

She was still up on the mountain. But where was her attacker? Where were Seth, Cassie and the others? Moving her eyes first, then her head, she craned to see. When her neck twinged, suggesting that she'd pulled muscles in the struggle, she winced and moved her body instead.

Or rather, she tried to move her body. It didn't budge, because she was tied fast.

Panic slapped through the mist of unreality, warning her that the situation was very, very real. Her heartbeat accelerated and her blood fired in her veins, telling her to run far and fast.

Or stand and fight.

Slow down, she told herself when her mind started to race in terror. *Think it through.* For some reason, she heard the last three words in Fax's voice. Instead of making her mad or sad, as it probably should have, the sound steadied her. It made her think of his warm, solid body and the mask he could drop over his eyes, making it seem like he was running cold when she knew from experience that the blood running in his veins was very, very hot.

She closed her eyes and pictured him, imagining the worry lines that cut beside his mouth from having taken on too much weight for far too long, and the unexpected dimple that winked on one cheek on the rare occasion when he smiled for real.

Holding that image in her mind, she consciously slowed her breathing and counted her heartbeats.

The panic receded somewhat. It was still there, no doubt about it. But it was manageable, more or less. She could think. She could plan.

Okay, she thought, opening her eyes. *What's the deal?*

Unfortunately, calming down hadn't improved her immediate situation much. She wasn't in danger of hyperventilating anymore, but she was still bound to a big tree at the edge of the landslide.

Worse, she could see a heavy work boot sticking out from behind the precarious tilt of the earthen overhang.

She recognized it as one of Tucker's boots. As she watched, it moved, swinging from side to side as though he was fighting the same sort of bonds she was.

Her heart seized on the sight and she gave a low cry of horror.

A masculine chuckle—low and nasty—greeted her response, and Muhammad stepped around in front of her, moving gingerly on the shifting soil at the edge of the slide.

He looked at her for a long moment, his eyes blatantly lingering on her breasts then flashing back to her face as though daring her to say something, challenging her to a fight she couldn't possibly win.

When she said nothing, merely glared at him with all the hatred that pounded in her veins, he sneered and turned his attention to the overhang. "You should've died that afternoon at your house, bitch. Then your friends wouldn't have gotten dragged into this." He fiddled with a small, flat handheld unit that might've been a PDA, might've been a phone, and said with a fake-sounding note of revelation, "Granted, then they probably would've been down at the stadium helping with crowd control and listening to that horrible excuse for a band. Which means they would've died anyway, once I did this."

Without warning, he lifted the handheld and pressed a couple of touch-pad keys.

"No!" Chelsea cried, realizing the unit was a detonator of some sort. "Don't!"

But it was already too late. There was a series of sharp explosions nearby, six of them, one after the other, *rat-tat-tat,* like machine-gun fire.

By themselves, they were little more than fire-crackers. Combined with the instability of the ground, though, they were devastating.

A low rumble started, humming in her bones and rising up through the audible wavelengths, shaking the tree she was bound to, making it sway and dip.

Looking surprised that the earth shift was fanning that far out, Muhammad shoved the unit in his pocket and started backing up, moving quickly but carefully. When he reached stabler ground, he sketched a wave in Chelsea's direction. "Bye, bitch. I hope it hurts."

The hatred vibrated in the air between them, less because of what she'd done to complicate al-Jihad's plans and more because of what she was—an American and a woman.

Her stomach twisted in knots at the thought that Muhammad, and men like him, were going to win this time.

The tree shuddered, dipping alarmingly, and

she cried out. Her words were lost beneath the growing roar, and suddenly the world was moving around her, underneath her. The overhang gave way and crashed like a breaking wave, sending tons of earth and rock onto the place where she'd seen Tucker's foot.

Chelsea screamed as her closest friends died. Tears blinded her and she choked on her sobs, on her terror. Then the earth was moving, faster and faster, gaining mass and momentum as it went, crashing its way toward the stadium. And Fax.

"Jonah!" she screamed, knowing there was nobody up on the mountain with her anymore who cared about her cries, except to feel pleasure in her pain.

Then the tree she was bound to pulled free of its root system, or the earth gave way beneath it, she wasn't sure which, she only knew that she was moving, tilting, and starting to slide, then stopping again as the entire mountainside paused, teetering on a pinpoint of balance that she knew could give way at any second.

Tears poured down her face. "*Jonah!*" she screamed again, even though she knew there was no hope of an answer.

Yet incredibly, she got one.

"Chelsea!" He was suddenly there, appearing out of nowhere, his face streaked with mud and sweat and set with horrible tension as he skidded along beside the tree she was tied to, yanking at her bonds. "Hang on!"

"What—" she gasped. "How?"

"Long story." He met her eyes briefly, and she saw a light in them that hadn't been there before, a mix of anger and something else, something that was simultaneously softer and hotter than his usual expression. "Short version is that you were right and I was wrong, but I'm not apologizing. I'm telling you I love you instead."

He gave a huge yank and the ropes came free.

Heart pounding from surprise and fear, and more adrenaline than she'd ever weathered in her life, she threw herself against him. *"Jonah!"*

He grabbed on to her, held her hard and started dragging her up and across the mountain face, moving fast, not seeming to care that the earth sponged and fell free beneath them, that their mad dash for safety was triggering small land-slides that merged into bigger ones.

"Hurry," he urged, dragging her along. "We've got to get out of here before—"

A huge freight-train roar cut him off, and the side of the mountain collapsed onto itself, and hurtled down the slope toward Bear Claw.

"Up here!" Jonah dragged her up onto a huge rock ledge, one that shuddered but held as the earth and smaller rocks pounded past it. He pulled her up, wrapped his arms around her, and held on so tightly she couldn't breathe.

She hugged him back just as tight, crying. "Jonah, the others…" she managed between sobs. "They were under the ledge when it gave."

He said something that she didn't catch, sure it was the roar of the avalanche. "What?"

Putting his lips close to her ear, he said, "They weren't under the ledge. I got them free while you distracted Muhammad. I sent them down the hill and told them to—" He broke off as a new sound echoed above the freight-train rumble, a heavy thump of detonations, one after the other, not the *rat-tat-tat* that had started the landslide, but the deep throated *whump-whump-whump* of heavy-duty explosives.

A cloud of earth shot up into the sky at the leading edge of the slide, and the avalanche changed course, flattening and dropping off, fanning out and eventually stopping.

The terrible roar diminished to a hiss, then a scattering of pebbles.

Chelsea stared, mouth agape. Then she turned to Fax, hardly able to believe what had just happened.

"You sent them to blast a channel between the slide and the stadium," she said in wonder.

He followed her gaze. "Looks like it worked."

"You let them go," she said and started to shake. "You took care of them first before you came for me."

Fax stiffened against her. "That doesn't mean—"

"No, no." She shushed him with her lips on his, letting him feel the smile in her kiss. "You trusted them to get the job done, and you trusted me to stay alive long enough for you to come for me. You did it right, Jonah. You saved us all."

A shudder went through his big body. "I almost didn't."

She heard him clearly, heard the pain and fear in his voice, because the landslide had trailed all the way to silence, piling into the trench her friends had blasted using explosives from the lower Quonset hut.

"But you did. Thank you." She pressed her lips to his, and he hesitated only a moment before he leaned into the kiss, opening to her and—

The click of a semiautomatic weapon being racked for firing echoed on the suddenly still air, freezing them both. Only for a second though, because before Chelsea could react, before she could even process the fact that they were in danger, Fax had twisted, bearing her to the ground and covering her as a bullet whistled over them both.

Then Fax lunged up with a roar, and charged Muhammad, who must've come back to make certain she was dead. As Fax came, he scooped up a handful of clay. Chelsea saw him grab Muhammad's gun with the hand that held the soil. Then Fax let go and danced away.

Al-Jihad's second in command roared something in a language Chelsea didn't know, spun toward Fax and fired point-blank.

The bullet impacted the pebbles and clay Fax had jammed down the barrel, and the weapon roared and jammed, blowing back in the terrorist's hands. He screamed and grabbed for his wrist as it spurted blood, and Fax took him down with a roundhouse to the jaw.

Muhammad went sprawling, bleeding and howling and clutching at his injured hand.

Fax kicked the gun away and then stood, breathing hard, staring down at his fallen enemy.

Chelsea gave the deep lacerations a quick look, and glanced at Fax. "He won't bleed out as long as he keeps pressure on."

"Then we'll tie him so he can." With more expediency than gentleness, Fax bound the sobbing man hand and foot, and searched him, dumping the contents of Muhammad's pockets into his own.

Seeing the transfer, Chelsea arched an eyebrow. "You planning on sharing that with the cops?"

Fax stilled, then turned slowly, that cool blankness dropping down to shield his expression, although she sensed that his blood was running hot and hard beneath. "Jane betrayed me—she was working for al-Jihad all along. Which means there may not be any way for me to prove my story, and even if I can, the authorities could still decide I'm a liability and a criminal." He drew a deep breath. "What if I said my next stop was Mexico?"

If it was a test, it was the easiest one Chelsea had ever taken. "Then I'd ask if I could swing by my place for a bathing suit."

He straightened, crossing to her and taking her hands in his, fitting their fingers together. "And if I said I wanted to turn myself in and offer up evidence against Jane in exchange for WitSec protection?"

She swallowed, knowing this was it, this was the rest of her life, staring at her with cool blue eyes that hid nothing of his feelings, once she knew where to look. "Then I'd ask if I could say goodbye to my friends before we left." Her voice shook a little on the words as she continued, "How about you? What's your opinion of taking on a most likely unemployed, blackballed medical examiner who's wishing she'd gone on that FBI interview way back when? For that matter, given that WitSec would make me change jobs anyway, what's your opinion of being with someone who suddenly doesn't know what she wants to be when she grows up?"

He inhaled a long, shuddering breath, then blew it out slowly so that he was almost whispering when he said, "I can't think of anything I'd like more. Employed, unemployed, spy, doctor, pathologist…I don't care what you wind up doing next, as long as I'm part of it." He dropped his forehead to hers. "I love you, Chelsea. We'll figure out the rest of it together, okay?"

Hope bloomed inside her, hard and hot, expanding to fill every inch of her body as she nodded, feeling her smile stretch so wide it pulled at the skin of her face as she rubbed her cheek against his, against the place where that elusive dimple flickered to life. "I love you back, Jonah. And, yeah, the rest will wait. This won't." She turned her lips to his, inviting a kiss, demanding it.

He'd just groaned and opened to her when a Bear Claw PD chopper buzzed up from below and hovered right above them, tilting to give its occupants a clear view.

Hoots and hollers filtered down, and Chelsea felt a laugh bubble up as she raised her hand and waved at her friends. "Guess they made it okay," she said, counting five heads pressed together in the windows. "And I'm guessing at least someone in the PD is grateful for our help. They sent the chopper after all."

Fax straightened away from her, although he kept an arm looped protectively around her waist as he surveyed the helicopter. She saw him look at the tree line as though considering making a break for it, and she elbowed him in the ribs. "Don't even think of it. These are my friends."

He looked at her for a long moment unspeaking, then nodded. "Mine, too, if they'll have me." He raised a hand to the chopper, gesturing for them to throw down a line, as there was nowhere to land.

And as he hooked them in and they were lifted up into the sky, Chelsea, who'd never been a big fan of heights, clung to his solid bulk and watched the ground fall away, knowing that as long as she was with him, she could do anything. Even fly.

The exultation was short-lived, though, because her friends weren't the only ones in the chopper—there was also a grim-faced man who immediately grabbed Fax and engaged him in low-voiced conversation, somehow isolating the two of them even in the crowded quarters of the helicopter.

The moment they touched down near the

stadium, that same man whisked Fax away into a dark sedan with tinted windows and government plates.

Fax didn't look back as the vehicle pulled away. And in the days that followed, he didn't call. There was no word of him, not even a rumor.

It was as if he'd disappeared.

Chapter Fourteen

It was three long, agonizing weeks before Fax's boots hit Colorado soil once again.

The last time he'd arrived in the Bear Claw area, he'd been cuffed and flanked by blank-faced U.S. Marshals, who he suspected would've shot to kill and enjoyed it, believing that he'd tortured and murdered two FBI agents.

This time he was alone and dressed in casual civilian clothes. The jeans and button-down shirt still felt a little strange after living so long in prison clothes.

He was carrying a duffel bag filled with new clothes, because when he'd gone back to the storage unit he'd rented right after Abby's death, the things inside the musty garage-size box had looked tired and irrelevant. So he'd picked out a few boxes of stuff he thought he might want some day and donated the rest to a local shelter.

Then he'd cleaned out his offshore bank

account, which had grown fat with the undercover pay Jane had funneled there through a shell company, and used the money to buy some essentials during the few breaks he'd been allowed between debriefings.

Those breaks had been few and far between. The grim-faced agents in charge hadn't outright refused to let him leave the bunkerlike maze of rooms located beneath an innocuous-looking building in downtown D.C. They'd made it clear, though, that the more he stayed put and answered the same questions over and over again, the higher his likelihood of making it out of there with some hope of a continued career within federal law enforcement.

He'd stayed and he'd given up everything he knew or even suspected about the op that he'd thought had been designed to draw out al-Jihad's conspirators, but had really been intended solely to help the murderer escape from the ARX Supermax prison. He told them everything, not because he wanted his career back, but because his main motivation for having entered the world in the first place remained unchanged. He wanted to help bring down al-Jihad and others like him, who attacked U.S. politics by killing noncombatants: women and children. Families.

Out of necessity, the info flow hadn't just been one way. The agents questioning Fax had revealed that al-Jihad and Lee Mawadi remained at large, as did Jane Doe. Worse, she had managed to use her equipment to feed misinformation to the cops on duty along the parade route.

That, combined with the chaos at the stadium and the lack of manpower on the mountain, meant that not only had all of al-Jihad's men escaped— with the exception of Muhammad, who was staying grimly tight-lipped so far—the conspirators remained undetected.

For a time, the investigation had focused on FBI agent Michael Grayson, the man who had arrested Fax in the stadium the day before the attack. Even more damning than his seemingly not-so-coincidental presence at the stadium, was that he'd also been the point of failure for a carefully worded warning sent by Seth Varitek early on the morning of the parade.

Grayson had received the information, determined it was a prank, and unilaterally decided not to add the manpower Varitek had suggested. In doing so, he had very nearly helped doom thousands of Bear Claw residents.

Despite that sign of complicity, a thorough investigation turned up no evidence that Grayson was linked to al-Jihad or any other terrorist. Instead, it turned out that the agent was suffering through the tail end of a very nasty divorce and had been living on caffeine pills rather than sleep or food.

Not surprisingly, he'd been pulled out of the field and would undergo major reviews and potentially lose his fieldwork status. But while it was a good thing to deal with an agent on the edge, with Grayson cleared of suspicion, they were left with few theories and even fewer clues regarding the structure of al-Jihad's terror cells or the where-abouts of the terrorist leader, Jane Doe or Lee Mawadi.

One of their few leads was Lee Mawadi's ex-wife who lived in a remote area roughly between Bear Claw and the ARX Supermax prison. She had divorced him shortly after his arrest for the Santa Bombings, claiming not to have had any idea of his criminal involvement. She'd quit her job as a magazine photographer and changed her name and had all but gone into seclusion in an isolated cabin high in the mountains. All of which was consistent with her claim that she hated her ex…except for the fact that her cabin was less than thirty miles from the prison.

If she had wanted to completely separate herself from her ex-husband…why had she chosen to live a short drive away from where he'd been incarcerated?

When asked, she'd told agents it was atonement, a reminder of the terrible mistake she'd made. Living near the peak of a low mountain, within sight of both the prison and Bear Claw City, she was constantly reminded of the people who'd died in the Santa Bombings.

Maybe she was telling the truth, maybe not. Regardless, the feds were keeping her under very tight surveillance.

The task force dedicated to bringing al-Jihad down was being headed up by a no-nonsense career agent named M. K. O'Reilly. There were still major questions of who could and couldn't be trusted, but Fax's gut said O'Reilly was clean. Then again, he'd missed the signs that Jane had turned. In retrospect it was far too easy to pick up on the little hints, the small inconsistencies, and the way she'd progressively cut him off from all his other contacts, until he'd been dealing with her and her alone.

He was furious with himself for being oblivious to the clues. Oddly, though, Jane's betrayal— not just of him but of the country he'd dedicated his life to protecting—didn't kick him back into the black hole of distrust he'd occupied in the months after Abby's death, the pit Jane herself had rescued him from.

Instead, he was able to hate Jane for the betrayal without hating himself, without withdrawing from the people around him.

That was Chelsea's doing, he knew. Any time the blackness encroached on his soul, he thought of her smile, her gentle sanity, and the way their hands had fit together, the way *they* had fit, even though on paper they never should've worked.

At least he'd told himself over and over that they worked, holding it as a lifeline, a mantra when things had looked their worst, when the grim-faced agents had hinted that he should plan for an extended stay, another incarceration, this time without the luxury of knowing deep down inside that he was one of the good guys, that he didn't belong there.

Then one day the threats had disappeared. In their place had been a job offer and an open door.

He was a free man now. He could dress how he wanted, could go where he wanted.

Which was what had brought him to Bear Claw.

When he got there, though, he pulled his rental over to the side of the road beside the *Welcome to Bear Claw City!* sign at the outskirts of the metro area.

And he sat there, wondering whether he'd blown it by not calling Chelsea in the intervening weeks, not letting her know where everything stood. The thing was, he hadn't wanted to call until he knew he was going to be able to come back to her.

"Well, you're back," he said to himself, staring up at the welcome sign. "Time to do your worst and hope for the best."

Still, it was a long time before he started driving again, and when he did his pulse was kicking, because for the first time in a long, long time, he was going to lay his heart—rather than his life—on the line.

For the first time in a long, long time, he cared.

More than that, he loved. He'd told her before, in the heat of the moment. Now it was time to see if she'd really meant it…because he sure as hell had.

SITTING IN HER small office in the ME's complex, Chelsea took another long look at the e-mail that had dropped into her computer's in-box. The return address was a government system, and there was an official seal at the upper left of the letter itself. The words *congratulations* and *please report* swam before her eyes, which misted at the realization that she was being offered a second chance at her dreams.

One of them, anyway. The other one appeared to be long gone, damn him.

Anger and heartache scratched at the back of her throat and she would've cursed herself for thinking of Fax. But if she started doing that, her days were likely to turn into a never-ending string of four-letter words, because she couldn't get him out of her head or her heart.

He'd swept into her life, turned her safe little universe upside down, told her he loved her and made her love him, and then disappeared without a word.

Jerk, she thought for the thousandth time and tried to find the anger that had sustained her for the first couple of weeks. It'd faded, though, leaving sadness behind—for herself, because she wanted the life they could've made together and for him because he'd been unable to break free of the patterns and beliefs that had bound him for too long. He was stuck in the past.

Well, not me, she thought, reading through the e-mail for the third time, finally beginning to believe she'd actually been accepted into the FBI's initial round of candidate screening.

She wasn't a shoo-in by any means, but she'd taken the first step.

"I have good news and bad news," she said when she heard someone come through the door, assuming it was Sara because she'd just called over and left a voice mail telling her boss that they needed to talk.

"Me, too," said a voice that was definitely *not* Sara's.

Chelsea froze. Then she looked up from her

monitor, moving slowly, half convinced that he'd disappear, proving to be the same figment she'd imagined too many times to count.

But he didn't disappear. He stayed put, with one shoulder propped against the door frame, his arms crossed over his chest, his forearms bare where he'd rolled up the sleeves of a crisp blue button-down shirt.

The shirt was jarring in its very normalcy, as were his new-looking jeans and belt, which seemed to be trying to make him look like a regular guy. They failed, though, because there was nothing average about his solid build and angular face or the powerful emotion in his eyes when he looked at her.

Chelsea's breath went thin in her lungs as she stood and moved around the desk to approach him.

Stopping just outside his reach, she lifted her chin. "What's your news?"

"You first," he said, challenging her. Teasing her.

And at that moment she knew it was going to be okay. She didn't know where he'd been, but in that instant she knew he'd come back for her, and this time he was there to stay. She knew because she could finally see the warmth in his eyes, the love.

Her heart beat double time beneath her skin

with a powerful combination of nerves and excitement. "I reapplied to the FBI and they've invited me to D.C."

"Of course they did. They're not stupid." The way he said it made her wonder whether he'd had something to do with the quick response. "What's the bad news?"

Her elation dimmed slightly. "It means leaving Sara in the lurch. With Jerry and Ricky both gone, she's shorthanded as it is. Worse, Mayor Proudfoot wants to replace her with someone more susceptible to pressure. He's leaning hard on IAD to investigate the office." She took a deep breath, then let it out. "But Sara's tough. She can take care of herself."

When she said it that way, it seemed obvious. Why had it taken her so long to figure out that she had to let go sometimes?

She tilted her head, taking a long look at the man who'd helped teach her that, by showing her the extreme of what could happen to a person who tried to take the world's problems on his shoulders and forgot to have his own life in the process.

"What about you?" she said, feeling her whole body shimmer with the warmth of his nearness, with the certainty that he'd come back for her. "What's your good news?"

"I'm here," he said simply, "and I'm staying. Not in Bear Claw, necessarily, but wherever you are. That's where I want to be."

He took her hand in his, and their fingers fit perfectly.

She stepped into him, leaned into him. "What's the bad news?"

"Same thing. Whether it's good news or bad depends on your perspective." He took her other hand, folded his fingers around hers and raised her knuckles to his lips. "That's assuming that you're willing to forgive me for taking a few weeks to get things squared away and make sure I didn't have to write you from the ARX Supermax, and you're happy to see me and you still want us to be together. In that case, then it's good news."

His eyes said he already knew what her answer would be, as did the touch of his lips against hers, bringing heat and want.

"And if I'm not willing to forgive?" she said against his mouth, letting go of his hands to wrap her arms around his waist, anchoring herself to his strength.

"Then it's bad news, because I have no intention of giving up what we could have together. I don't care how long it takes, I'm going to stick it out and make it work." His eyes were intent on hers. "So, which is it? Good news or bad?"

She smiled as the warmth that'd gathered in her heart moved outward, radiating through her body like need. Like love. "Oh, it's good news. Very, very good news."

And as they kissed, twining together in her office doorway, she knew that no matter where she chose to go from here, what she chose to do, she wouldn't be doing it alone. She had a partner now. A lover.

A friend.

* * * * *

Don't miss the next book in Jessica Andersen's
BEAR CLAW CREEK CRIME LAB
miniseries in early 2009,
only from Harlequin Intrigue!

Here's a sneak peek at
THE CEO'S CHRISTMAS PROPOSITION,
the first in USA TODAY *bestselling author*
Merline Lovelace's HOLIDAYS ABROAD
trilogy coming in November 2008.

American Devon McShay is about to get the Christmas surprise of a lifetime when she meets her new client, sexy billionaire Caleb Logan, for the very first time.

Silhouette
Desire

Available November 2008

Her breath whistled out in a sigh of relief when he exited Customs. Devon recognized him right away from the newspaper and magazine articles her friend and partner Sabrina had looked up during her frantic prep work.

Caleb John Logan, Jr. Thirty-one. Six-two. With jet-black hair, laser-blue eyes and a linebacker's shoulders under his charcoal-gray cashmere overcoat. His jaw-dropping good looks didn't score him any points with Devon. She'd learned the hard way not to trust handsome heartbreakers like Cal Logan.

But he was a client. An important one. And she was willing to give someone who'd served a hitch in the marines before earning a B.S. from the University of Oregon, an MBA from Stanford and his first million at the ripe old age of twenty-six the benefit of the doubt.

Right up until he spotted the hot-pink pashmina, that is.

Devon knew the flash of color was more visible than the sign she held up with his name on it. So she wasn't surprised when Logan picked her out of the crowd and cut in her direction. She'd just plastered on her best businesswoman smile when he whipped an arm around her waist. The next moment she was sprawled against his cashmere-covered chest.

"Hello, brown eyes."

Swooping down, he covered her mouth with his.

Sheer astonishment kept Devon rooted to the spot for a few seconds while her mind whirled chaotically. Her first thought was that her client had downed a few too many drinks during the long flight. Her second, that he'd mistaken the kind of escort and consulting services her company provided. Her third shoved everything else out of her head.

The man could kiss!

His mouth moved over hers with a skill that ignited sparks at a half dozen flash points throughout her body. Devon hadn't experienced that kind of spontaneous combustion in a while. A *long* while.

The sparks were still popping when she pushed off his chest, only now they fueled a flush of anger.

"Do you always greet women you don't know with a lip-lock, Mr. Logan?"

A smile crinkled the skin at the corners of his eyes. "As a matter of fact, I don't. That was from Don."

"Huh?"

"He said he owed you one from New Year's Eve two years ago and made me promise to deliver it."

She stared up at him in total incomprehension. Logan hooked a brow and attempted to prompt a nonexistent memory.

"He abandoned you at the Waldorf. Five minutes before midnight. To deliver twins."

"I don't have a clue who or what you're…"

Understanding burst like a water balloon.

"Wait a sec. Are you talking about Sabrina's old boyfriend? Your buddy, who's now an ob-gyn doc?"

It was Logan's turn to look startled. He recovered faster than Devon had, though. His smile widened into a rueful grin.

"I take it you're not Sabrina Russo."

"No, Mr. Logan, I am *not*."

* * * * *

Be sure to look for
THE CEO'S CHRISTMAS PROPOSITION
by Merline Lovelace.
Available in November 2008 wherever books
are sold, including most bookstores,
supermarkets, drugstores and discount stores.

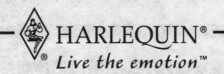

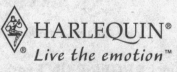

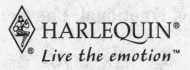

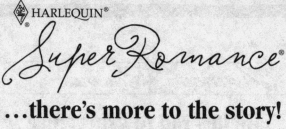
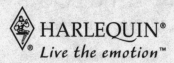

HARLEQUIN®
Presents

The world's bestselling romance series...
The series that brings you your favorite authors,
month after month:

Helen Bianchin...Emma Darcy
Lynne Graham...Penny Jordan
Miranda Lee...Sandra Marton
Anne Mather...Carole Mortimer
Melanie Milburne...Michelle Reid

and many more talented authors!

Wealthy, powerful, gorgeous men...
Women who have feelings just like your own...
The stories you love, set in exotic, glamorous locations...

HARLEQUIN®
Presents

Seduction and Passion Guaranteed!

HPDIR08

www.eHarlequin.com

Harlequin® Historical
Historical Romantic Adventure!

Imagine a time of chivalrous knights and unconventional ladies, roguish rakes and impetuous heiresses, rugged cowboys and spirited frontierswomen— these rich and vivid tales will capture your imagination!

Harlequin Historical . . . they're too good to miss!

HHDIR06

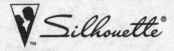

Silhouette®

SPECIAL EDITION™

Emotional, compelling stories that capture the intensity of living, loving and creating a family in today's world.

Modern, passionate reads that are powerful and provocative.

Dramatic and sensual tales of paranormal romance.

Silhouette® Romantic SUSPENSE

Romances that are sparked by danger and fueled by passion.